CARYL PHILLIPS

Higher Ground

Caryl Phillips was born in 1958 in St. Kitts, West Indies, and went with his family to England that same year. He was brought up in Leeds and educated at Oxford. He has written numerous scripts for film, theater, radio and television; *The European Tribe*, a book of nonfiction that won the 1987 Martin Luther King Memorial Prize; and five novels, including *Cambridge*.

INTERNATIONAL

Higher Ground

CARYL PHILLIPS

Higher Ground

A Novel in Three Parts

Vintage International

Vintage Books

A Division of Random House, Inc.

New York

For My Mother

First Vintage International Edition, November 1995

Copyright © 1989 by Caryl Phillips

Library of Congress Cataloging-in-Publication Data
Phillips, Caryl.
Higher ground: a novel in three parts / Caryl Phillips.
p. cm.
ISBN 0-679-76376-7
I. Title.
[PR9275.S263P4764 1995]
823'.914–dc20 95-14371
CIP

Author photograph © Jerry Bauer

Manufactured in the United States of America
10 9 8 7 6 5 4 3 2 1

Lord plant my feet on higher ground

TRADITIONAL

CONTENTS

I

Heartland

9

I I

The Cargo Rap

61

I I I

Higher Ground

173

I

Heartland

kiss me but I turn my head from him and the tears come easily and naturally. I am ashamed, for they are tears of joy and gratitude. I want him to hug me tight. He strokes my hair and pulls my head down on to his chest and I want to lie down with this man for ever. Please let nobody disturb this serenity. I awaken from my dream and smash a mosquito against my leg. Loneliness scales the walls of my being and threatens to destroy my soul. Her assaults are increasingly difficult to withstand. Have all Gods abandoned me?

He clasps a camphor bag to his face and kicks open the door with his boot. The dungeon smells foul, the air thick with a putrefaction impossible to disguise. No amount of cleansing will ever make this place inodorous. I lean forward and thrust the lantern into the darkness so that he might see where he is stepping. A large black rat is caught in the light; erect, on its haunches, it stares for an instant, then scrambles for cover. I bump into the back of the man who has suddenly stopped dead in his tracks. 'Excuse me, sir.' He takes the lantern from me and swings it first left then right. The flame threatens to die. There is too little oxygen. I look behind me to make sure that the door is still open. It is. The man's lantern finds the rat's nest, a writhing mass of fetid fur and flashing teeth and eyes. 'They are everywhere,' I say in an attempt to comfort him. 'Down here they are more difficult to control because it is used so infrequently. It is easier in the men's lodgings and in the storehouses.' He nods as though trying to tell me to be quiet. I obey. He stands and looks about himself and then kicks at the neck-chains with his boots. They are solidly bolted into the earth. He is testing their strength. He hands me the lantern and falls on one knee where he begins to pull at the chains. They will defeat him, but I think he knows this. But still he pulls. At length he climbs to his feet and retrieves the lantern. In the corner trading equipment is temporarily stored: whips, flails, yokes, branding-irons, metal masks. 'How many?' he asks. 'How many in this cell?' I appropriate nonchalance. 'One hundred. Maybe one hundred and fifty.' His eyes do not stray from my face. 'We have four such dungeons.' I do not wish to alarm

15

him but I can see that he is concerned. 'It is not so bad,' I say. 'They do not stay here long. It is just a place of storage.' He reaches up and pushes at the stone ceiling with the flat of his hand. 'How long?' he asks. 'Days? Weeks? A month or two?' 'Weeks,' I reply. He points: 'And these markings?' I follow the line of his finger. 'Those with small pox, when they move they leave behind skin and blood. Then, of course, many have dysentery. Such stains are common.' He turns now to leave, but I must wait for him to lead the way. It is only proper. We stand outside and I lock back the door and push home both bolts. The light dazzles us and we shield our eyes. I extinguish the lantern. 'Men and women together?' What can I answer but the truth. 'No,' I say. 'Men and children together. Women often attempt to take their children's lives. They are kept separately. I believe it is the same everywhere. We are neither different from nor worse than any other trading post.' He must know this. I sigh inwardly. Why does he act the virgin with such vigour? I begin to not only distrust this man, but to dislike his feigned innocence. Such men are dangerous. 'Perhaps we should talk later.' It is as I feared. 'Perhaps you might report to my lodgings this evening.' It is a command framed in the form of a request. I simply wait for his departure, but he seems reluctant to leave me alone. I continue to stand and wait. 'I should have spoken with James.' The man walks away with the old Governor's name ringing loudly around his head.

The dreary afternoon langour consumes my energy. I creep up on to the ramparts and fold myself into an alcove. I doze off. I awake to voices. Price's voice is raised, his tones clipped and definite. I hear the sound of the Governor, firm but uncertain. The twin symphony of argument cuts through the somnambulance of the afternoon. I twist to the side and try to hear no more. It is their business.

Lewis stands over me. I think that his life here is only made tolerable by his feeling able to intermittently bestow gestures of kindness upon me. I have often wondered were there a dog or some stray animal in the Fort, whether Lewis would deem it a more appropriate receptacle into which to pour his compassion. But there are no animals (apart from the rats, of course). The taunting and torturing of creatures – particularly lizards – is an occupation that helps the soldiers to pass time. The dumb have learned that it is better for them to hold their curiosity at bay and remain outside the high stone walls. 'Thought I might find you up here. What are you doing then?' His words roll into and over each other. It is only recently that I have been able to comprehend his sentences. Prior to this I used to nod earnestly and hope that he was not asking a question which demanded a more formal reply. 'Well come on then.' He taps me with the toe of his boot. 'Get up, you old ragamuffin.' I unbuckle my body and realize that age is beginning to weather my bones and joints. I take his hand. He hoists me up until I fall about a foot below his own height. 'You can't stay up here all night. Better get you back down to your quarters, eh?' Lewis is a slender young man with features as yet unmarked by the coast. He stands awkwardly as if embarrassed by his height. His eyes follow mine. The distant sky is studded with stars. 'Not much to see out there, though they say the ship'll soon be here. Plenty to see and do then.' His voice is tinged with sorrow. 'I don't know,' he muses, 'one day I'm a thresher in a field in my native county, next day I'm standing here with you looking out over the ocean. Never know what's gonna happen to you. But I wouldn't mind seeing home again.' I continue to look out over the sea but I feel his eyes upon me. I try not to spend too much time talking with the young soldier, his friendship being too easily proffered for my own comfort. 'Come on then, I'll lead you back down to your quarters. You'll be alright with me.' We cross the courtyard and pass clusters of soldiers who silently greet Lewis, while others ignore him completely. I am no longer sure if they ignore him because of his junior status or because they know something about him that I am ignorant of. Lewis stops outside of the door to my small refuge. 'Right, I'll be leaving you then. Look after yourself and sleep tight. And don't be falling asleep up there again. Some of the boys ain't as easy going about such things as I am.' I try to look grateful, then I push open the door. Lewis peers in over my head.

'Bloody hell, a bit dark in there, ain't it?' I am anxious now. 'I get used to it.' He lets out a long low sigh. I watch as he turns and makes his way off into the night. Has he got any friends? Is this why he talks with me? Do they think him strange for talking with me? The dual discord of Price and the Governor begins to soar above the barrack-room clamour. My room is close to the Governor's lodgings. As their voices rise and fall I am able to determine the strength of each's argument, although I am unable to make out what it is they disagree about. Perhaps nothing, or perhaps the Governor is trying to impose some new changes upon the routine of the Fort. Price has the soldiers' interests at heart, the Governor those of the Company. I imagine at times they are one and the same interest, at other times not. Is this the basis for their shouting and noise? I strip off my shirt. These two men are not fighting each other but time and the coast. But still they persist. I lie down and try to conquer thoughts that send blood surging through my loins. To hold myself gives me warmth and some pleasure, but its basic perversity repels me. I would rather I had no such urges any more, that this thing in me could die so I would no longer have to service it with energy of mind and self-administered physical abuse. I must try and achieve some sleep if I am to maintain any sense of daily discipline. These days, through no fault of my own, I am left with little to occupy myself. I have to create my own routine. Rising in the morning and retiring in the evening provides me with the most basic of maps.

I cannot sleep. The noise from the Governor's lodgings is overpowering. I rise and silently cross the courtyard. I stand by his door, a blanket swathed around my shoulders to stave off the chill from the sea air. 'The company sent me here to do a job,' continues the Governor, 'and regardless of what you say it will be done.' 'But there are ways and means of doing things.' 'Yes,' interrupts the Governor, 'my ways!' It would appear that this is the sole logic behind their confrontation.

My world moves at the same regular pace, but suddenly the

world around me is injected with a new energy. No longer do the days snake endlessly towards sunset. There is purpose. The Fort looks smarter, uniforms are cleaner, swords brighter, and horses are being brushed down, their stirrups, braces and harnesses shined. I am grateful that the Governor has not made another request to see me. He seems to have forgotten his early desire to make me a confidant. I try hard to appear as though I am occupied with something of great import, although as ever there is little for me to do that is either constructive or useful. Within the confines of the Fort my position is secure, if low and often unbearable. I now find it difficult to conceive of a life either before or after this place. I need to feel safe. I sneak up on to the ramparts for my afternoon rest. Already Lewis is there. He squats with his back to the wall. As I walk towards him he looks at me; I imagine that he has been drinking. I stand over him and smell the liquor. He should not drink so much. 'Hey, you looking for me?' he begins. I shake my head. 'Well I'm looking for you.' I sit down next to him and sense that some violence is being played out in this youngster's soul. 'I'm not going,' he says. He mentions this boldly as though it is something to be proud of. 'I'm staying here with you and a few others to guard the Fort. They keep telling me it's a responsible job. I suppose it is in a way, isn't it, but I didn't come all the way out here to sit in the sun and sweat like a rotting apple. I want some action, otherwise what's the point of being young? You might as well just sit around waiting to get old. What do you think?' He laughs. He does not wish to know what I think. 'They're leaving me behind.' His voice is rich with disbelief. 'No offence to you, or the others, but it seems to me a waste of time, don't you think?' I look out over the littoral side of the Fort and wait for him to say more. A wave breaks; then a second and a third. He climbs unsteadily to his feet and faces me. 'Listen, Mr Price wants to see you. You better come along with me.' I suggest to Lewis that I should see Price on my own. He understands the undisguised helplessness of his own condition. 'Maybe,' muses Lewis. 'Don't know what he wants but be careful though. Crafty bugger, old Price.' Lewis slumps down again. His sword scrapes against the stone, his knees tuck up under his chin. Why am I beginning to feel sorry for this man? After all, regardless of the more obvious differences of our origins, we are all trapped by similar circumstances. We must confront them as best we can. Lewis cowers, his body bunched up, his mouth stinking with drink, and simply discharges his foolish concerns. Has he ever thought about my concerns? Is he even aware that people such as I have concerns? The stupid little boy. I stand and walk across to the wall. Lewis looks up at me. 'You had better go,' he says. I know this, but some reasoning in my brain wants to force him into a despotic position, one which will give me an unchallengeable excuse to dislike him. Who does he imagine he is talking to? This young boy who has done nothing with his life, who has fathered no children, who has no history of supporting himself (let alone others). Does he know to whom he is talking? I step past him and feel his heavy eyes following me. 'Good luck!' he cries. 'Thank you,' I reply.

Price sits behind his desk. I suspect he is not familiar with the ritual. Perhaps this is at the source of their conflict, one man considering himself the intellectual superior of the other. Such conflicts are commonly draped in simple images: a desk is a simple image. The surface of this desk is empty. It supports Price's two elbows, his cupped palms support his chin. His stare is intense, his intention to reduce me to a state of uneasiness. 'Sit down.' As he speaks the whole head moves up and down. 'You will take me to the nearest village. This is something between you and I, nothing the Governor need be aware of, do you understand me?' I nod. 'Once there we will conduct our business swiftly. There will be no further mention of whatever it is you might see.' Again I nod. Price stands up. He is a thick-set man in his late thirties, a graduate of the coast, a man who I imagine back in his own country would have held a similar position of bullying authority. He seems to me a man who knows his own mind and there is safety in this. He stands straight; he fixes me with a clear eye; he makes his decisions without deliberation. 'I will be ready to leave in the morning. Just you and I. Meet me here at dawn.' Again I nod.

I understand. I leave Price and try all the while to imagine his country. Is it so distinct from here? More people perhaps, bigger rivers, a different heat? It is often difficult to understand these people. Perhaps the answers lie in their world. I will one day find the courage to ask more. Until then I go about my day-to-day business with the sedulity of a man who knows what is good for him.

I cannot sleep. I rise from my fitful fretting and leave my quarters. I cross the courtyard and find myself outside the Governor's door. His sentry is asleep. In my madness I push at the door and enter his chamber. The Governor is sprawled across the bed, his face lined with disquiet. What is occupying this man's mind? What awful secret is he harbouring? He promised me his confidence. He walked me around the courtyard in full view of the others. He risked his own credibility by doing so. And now he divorces himself from me. I watch him until through the window I see fresh light streaking the sky and I know that I must prepare myself for the adventure of a new day.

'Did your people ever wage war with the people of this village?' Price turns to face me. He seems anxious now. Our two horses amble across the vast open tract. They remain close, as though yoked together. 'We never waged war of any kind. The Head Man in our village was a peace-loving man, and respected among the whole community. It was he who taught us that such things as war were not in the interests of our people. He preached moderation.' We ride on together. I still do not know what is expected of me. Occasionally Price stops to relieve himself. He makes no attempt at discretion. He no doubt feels that somebody of my assumed bestiality will not be shocked by his animalistic behaviour, but I turn my head. Each time we resume our journey a silence clouds the atmosphere. I can only conjecture that he is aware that I stare in the other direction and this disturbs him. I do not mind. I simply wait for him to raise his objection. We press on. The sun is high. The plains stretch away for miles and give no clue of human or animal life. I look for birds but, there are none. Price does not appear to notice how ominous this is. He is totally occupied with his task of reaching the nearest village. As the years pass by the nearest village moves further inland. I look from right to left and survey the horizon. Then again Price begins to talk. He asks me how many soldiers there are stationed at the Fort. I tell him I do not know. I guess. 'Perhaps fifty, maybe more?' 'Thirty-seven,' he says and laughs. 'We need seventy, eighty at least.' 'Disease?' I suggest. Price looks straight ahead and again he laughs. He clearly has no intention of discussing this subject with me. We ride on in silence until the evanescent sun begins to set. Up ahead I see the low outline of a village at rest, a thin scarf of smoke the only signal of life. I point out the village to Price who seems pleased, yet at the same time I notice a look of worry. He does not know what to expect. He relaxes his pace until I am in the lead, my horse a whole body length in front of his, and this is how we pass through the stockade. The village is denuded. It contains mainly women and old men, with a few children (the seedlings) running wild. They will soon blossom into the young exportable goods of this trading continent. I ride, with Price at my rear, towards the Head Man, who comes out of his hut to greet us. He stands impassively. I can say nothing until I have been informed of what it is we are doing here. I stop in front of the Head Man, who raises his hand to greet us. I turn to Price. 'Is he friendly?' asks Price. I swallow in order to suppress my laughter. I wonder if Price understands irony? I inform him that I do not think we are in any danger from this old man. Price glares at me, but I continue. 'What would you like me to say to him?' Price does not answer. He looks around at the nakedness of the villagers. They stare back at my clothes and Price's person with similar disdain. It is moments such as these that I loathe. Marooned between them, knowing that neither fully trusts me, that neither wants to be close to me, neither recognizes my smell or my posture, it is only in such situations that the magnitude of my fall strikes me. I want to run. 'Tell him I need a young girl. She will be well treated and eventually returned. She will not go with the others.' I look at Price in disbelief. He stares back. I turn to the

22

Head Man and relay Price's request. I try to conjure as much indifference as possible. There is a long silence. Some women scamper off to warn others. Everyone in the village is being informed of the purpose of the intrusion, and already nobody believes that the girl will be returned. The silence deepens and I realize that the decision will not be immediately forthcoming. The Head Man encourages us to get down from our horses and share a drink. I tell this to Price. As our feet reach solid ground the horses are led away by an Elder to be rested and replenished. 'Come this way.' The Head Man beckons us into his hut. Price suggests that I go first for he is afraid (despite the fact that any hostile act would almost certainly bring about the destruction of this village). I enter. We sit cross-legged on the floor. I am positioned between the two men and Price asks me to explain to the Head Man the urgency of our expedition. I am to tell him that we must return as soon as possible otherwise there are those who might become agitated by our absence and act foolishly. The Head Man understands exactly what is being threatened but he merely smiles at Price. He sees a man beneath the uniform. He addresses Price. 'These things take time.' I convey this to Price, who says nothing. I can see that he suspects me of some complicity in this delay. We sit for two hours. The Head Man asks us about our journey, then composes questions for me to put to Price about his country and his people. Price fields them with thinly veiled impatience, continually encouraging me to ask again what they are doing about the girl. Sometimes I ask, sometimes I do not ask. I understand much better than Price the way in which these things work. To appear too desperate is foolish and will only slow down the process. So we talk on, and Price's face darkens. The Head Man stands. He smiles as he informs me that it will be possible for Price to have a girl, but the selection of the girl will not occur for at least another hour. There are things to be done. We must spend the night here. It will not be safe for us to travel back through the night. A place where the two of us might sleep is being prepared. Price launches into a crazed set of quiet objections. I tone down their substance, but to no avail. The Head Man looks at Price and laughs as though gently mocking a child. He

23

suggests that we should take a little rest. He thinks that our hut will be ready for us. We are led across the village by the Elder who serviced the horses. We enter a smaller and more modest hut. Once there Price informs me that I will have to remain outside and guard him. I had expected nothing different from this man. I sit outside and wait. Everyone who passes by leaves an excessive amount of room between themselves and the hut. It is only natural. Behind me I hear Price. I turn and look into the hut where he lies flat on his back, boots still on his feet, mouth half-open. He snores lightly. I decide to take a walk in an effort to make contact with somebody who might talk with me. I move no more than a few yards before the Elder appears as though from nowhere. He informs me not to stray. 'Your life will be in danger.' Then he spits in my face. 'You are filth. There are many old warriors in this village who would happily go to the Gods with your death on their hands.' I wipe away the spittle and choose not to retaliate. Why do they seem intent upon blaming me? Have I, unlike their Head Man, ever made profit for myself? I merely survive, and if survival is a crime then I am guilty. I have no material goods, no fine hut in which to dwell, nobody to wait on me. I set the circumstances of my existence against those of these Elders and I laugh. They are able to justify their way of life by pointing to people like myself whom they consider guilty of a greater betrayal. But observe the price of their treachery. Their sons and daughters are gone from them for ever. Yet I, who stayed behind, am expected to be something other than I am; which is an ordinary man doing an extraordinary job in difficult times. They blame me because I am easily identifiable as one who dwells with the enemy. But I merely oil the wheels of their own collaborationist activities. 'You stay where you are,' commands the Elder. I sit and wait and try hard not to throw my mind either backwards or forwards into new territory, for it is almost certain to be territory too painful to inhabit. Draining the mind is a tedious but necessary business. I am grateful, and would thank the Gods (if there were any to thank) that I have finally mastered this art of forgetting – of murdering the memory.

*

24

Again I sit between the Head Man and Price, this time around a blazing fire where a goat is being sacrificed. It is a great feast, and obviously food is being spent that was meant for a different and one assumes more important ceremony. Two men beat drums while another man plays on the flute. We eat heartily; I recall my youth and feel an overwhelming sense of loss. I tear at a piece of meat and await the climax of this festival. Price drinks wine as though it were water. I sense frustration searing through him. The Head Man stands and claps together his hands, and again Price whispers in my ear, 'Is this it?', and this time I am able to confirm that indeed it is. Six young girls, I guess their ages to be between thirteen and sixteen, are led forth draped in white cloths which give them an additional air of youth and innocence. Price's eyes light up and he asks what he should do. I shrug my shoulders and tell him that he must wait for the Head Man to pronounce upon the situation. The girls are marshalled into a straight line. The Head Man gestures towards the girls and announces that it is possible for Price to choose whichever one he wants. I relay the information to Price who stands and joins the Head Man. Neither one of them understands the words of the other. Again the Head Man gestures towards the girls and he and Price nod in unison; a comical performance. Price turns around and looks at me. He needs some clarification. I step forward and explain again that the Head Man wishes him to choose one of the girls. He asks me if there are any that he should avoid and I look at the girls and tell him that they all appear to be fine. He immediately chooses the fifth of the six girls, her hair cropped short, gold rings through both ears, and a murmur rises among the villagers. They seem shocked and Price turns to me and asks if he has committed an indiscretion; I cannot help him. His choosing of this girl has provoked some reaction but I do not understand why. The Head Man asks the girl to come forward; he kisses her on both cheeks and then pushes her so that she now faces Price. She is perhaps sixteen, probably the oldest of all the girls, and certainly the prettiest. Price grins and she lowers her eyes with well-practised modesty. He asks me, 'What next?' The Head Man claps his hands and all the girls, including Price's girl, disappear as magically as they had arrived. Then the Head Man sits and it is clear that we are expected to do the same. I sit and Price sits alongside me. The Head Man continues to eat. I can only guess at what happens next, for the Head Man seems totally occupied with slaking his hunger. 'We must finish our food and then retire to sleep. In the morning the girl will come with us.' This explanation seems to satisfy a healthier-looking Price. The Head Man looks across and smiles at the intruder. Price, his mouth full of meat, smiles back in a self-satisfied manner. They both laugh with, and maybe at, each other. I look at the space between my dusty feet and welcome the inarticulate contact that they are making. I wish that I could somehow slip away, but their communication does not last long. The wine that we are drinking is affecting Price. He rises unsteadily. I help him and look down at the Head Man. He says nothing. He merely points at the Elder who took our horses, the same man who spat in my face. The Elder comes to us and speaks; 'At dawn there will be three horses not two. Go in peace; look after the girl.' He leads us back to our hut and moves off without wishing us a good night. Price stands outside the hut and shakes his head; then he pats me on the back. 'Well done,' he says. But even as he speaks I can see the girl inside the hut. Price sees her and in his drunken stupor begins to laugh. I suggest that he should have her sleep outside the hut. 'It could cause trouble.' He leers at the girl and then growls at me. 'Well then why put her in there in the first place?' I sense that Price's attitude is becoming enveloped in a drunken bitterness. I say nothing and hope that common sense will overcome his desire for the girl. We stand facing each other. I am unable to back down having made a forceful case. Price realizes the strength of my position and orders me to lead the girl out of the hut. He instructs me brutally, with little generosity of spirit, then he walks away and sits and stares blankly into the night. The girl crouches in the corner of the hut and seems somewhat relieved that the face she is looking at is mine and not that of Price. I call to her, but stop when I realize that I am doing so in a tone of voice that one associates with the addressing of a pet animal. 'You will go back to your own hut tonight.' I find a firmness of voice more appropriate to the situation. She looks at me and gathers up her small bundle of belongings. I have more to say but she quickly pushes past me and disappears from my sight. There is only Price and I and the stars. I walk over to Price but he has fallen asleep. He snores heavily, not the light snoring of his previous slumber. It is a louder and more ugly sound. I know that to nudge him gently will have little effect. He has passed into a world where I would risk his wrath were I to rouse him. I back off and take up a position behind the hut where I too hope to fall asleep. I look at the sky and wonder about the manner in which I am being treated. I have cut myself off from these villagers to such an extent that I have actually become their enemy; perhaps my life is in danger? I decide that it is best that I do not sleep. They have tried to discover Price by putting the girl in with him, but they do not have to discover me for they know exactly who I am. I worry. And then the silver breast of moon begins to dissolve and a cerulean blue washes the sky as dawn breaks. I feel my eyelids closing.

A foot stabs at my side. I roll over and the sputum hits the dust where only seconds before my head lay. The Elder stands with three horses and the girl to his side. I am angry that he has attempted to humiliate me in front of her. 'Get up!' My bones and thin muscles ache from having had so little sleep and in such an ungainly position. He spits again and this time the spittle brushes my arm. I wipe it off and get to my feet. 'Where is your owner?' The Elder makes a deliberate attempt to anger me further. I wonder if he truly derives pleasure from such behaviour, or if this morning's performance is especially brutal in a quest to impress the girl. 'I have no owner.' I turn from them both. Price is inside the hut; he snores loudly. Perhaps he was placed there by villagers. I touch him but he does not stir. I push him. He opens his eyes and looks wildly around as though unaware of his location. He climbs to his feet and rubs the sleep from his face. 'Is everything alright?' I nod. He follows me out of the hut, and we stand before the girl and the Elder and the horses. The Elder touches the girl on the arm, a gesture of departure. Then he leaves. 'Do we have provisions for the day's journey?' asks Price. 'Water and some dried meat.' Price nods. I suggest that we depart. I explain to the girl that we are leaving, but she says nothing. I ask if she would like me to help her up and on to her horse, but again she says nothing. She mounts the horse in one neat bound and sits astride it like a man. She looks down haughtily at Price and myself. We both climb up on to our horses and I lead the procession out of the village. It would appear that everybody is awake, but nobody says anything. Women gather water and wash their children. Elders smoke their pipes and stare. We are the strangest of parties, and we are leaving for a different world before the sun has fully cleared the horizon. We have among us one who knows not what her fate is, but who has been guaranteed safety of passage by one who is not of them, and another who is in their eyes irredeemably tainted. I am sure their thoughts must be with the girl.

Occasionally we stop for water and in order that we might rest the horses. Then, of course, there is the averting of our eyes as the girl performs her bodily functions (although we never look to see if she affords us the same degree of privacy when it is our turn to perform). We ride on and hope that our queer party will reach its destination in peace. It is rumoured that there remain wandering bands of marauders who would kill both Price and myself, for there is much honour to be gained in taking our lives and perhaps liberating the girl. Although the risk is small we proceed with caution, our eyes sweeping the plains for signs of any untoward movement, but we see nothing. At noon we find shelter under a tree and drink water. Price takes the lion's share of the dried meat. He eats hungrily. The girl sits cross-legged, her long legs spread out on either side like butterfly wings; she eats with slow deliberation. She will not be rushed. A fly buzzes around her head but she does not flinch. She seems happy to see it land and walk all over her body. Perhaps she has accepted the logic of peaceful coexistence. The fly does not enjoy aimless buzzing any more than she enjoys spinning her hands around in large unnecessary circles trying to knock it out of the air. I finish my food. Price stands ready to depart. I stand and join him, but the girl ignores us. Price glares at me as though I am responsible for this act of rebellion, but I stare back and invite him to give me some instructions. He says nothing. Price sits back down and takes another drink. It would appear that he is prepared to wait, so I too sit. The girl looks at neither of us and seems totally oblivious to this drama of waiting. I do not know whether to admire or abhor her for this ostentatious display of self-control. Again Price climbs to his feet, and this time he makes it clear that he expects me to speak with her. I am expected to tell her that we must leave now for Price wishes to depart. For the first time I find myself faced with the problem of how to label Price. Her master? Perhaps I should describe him as the 'deputy', but clearly she is ignorant of what he is the deputy of; such labels make little sense unless one is also sure about the deputy's superior. 'Deputy' both inflates and reduces Price. I call him 'the man'. 'The man wishes to go now.' She gets to her feet. With one skilful leap she is aboard her horse and ready to leave. And so our party moves off again. By no means do I feel totally revived, for it has been a long and hard journey. I know that it will soon be over but cannot help feeling that this last twenty-four hours has marked the beginning of the end of a period in my life. Something has changed. Possibly my own sense of despair; it may have deepened.

As we near the Fort I see the flags flying above it. I look across at the girl, who for the first time seems troubled. I think it unusual that she has not ventured to ask me (in our own language) the meaning behind her journey. (Perhaps it is as well; I would not have been able to give her a satisfactory answer.) She dwells in ignorance. Perhaps she has decided that the less she knows the safer it will be for her, a mode of thought that is alien to the man who has made this pilgrimage. He (and others like him) does not possess the inner stillness that I have noticed as a trait of our people: they are for ever curious, unable to remain in a state of tranquillity for any length of time. But that is their way. The gates swing open and we pass through and into the courtyard where a small crowd of soldiers gather to greet Price and take his horse to be watered. I dismount, after the triumphant Price, but the girl remains mounted. She looks straight ahead as though unaware that all eyes are upon her. It is some time since a native woman last entered the Fort. (They have forgotten what their own women look like.) The men relieve their sexual boredom in whatever base and private ways they can devise, or wait until the time when the Fort is full and then pluck and plunder until their disease-ridden bodies can neither take nor give any more. They stare at the girl but she continues to look out far beyond their gaze and reveal little. The small knot of soldiers part and the Governor steps forward. He is attired in full military uniform. It appears to me unwise, for even at this late afternoon hour the sun remains unrepentant. Price extends a hand which the Governor refuses to shake. The Governor looks up at the girl as Price attempts to solve the problem of what to do with his now foolish hand. 'Mr Price, what is the meaning of this?' The Governor speaks in a low voice, the tremor barely concealed. Price says nothing. He turns to one of the soldiers and requests that the girl be taken to his quarters where materials should be provided for her to wash herself. I fully expect the Governor to protest but he says nothing and the girl is led off in silence. The soldiers drift away and the two men face each other. Those stubborn enough to remain are soon dispersed by the Governor. 'What are you men waiting for? Move!' I too begin to move, and I think of how sweet the matting and straw in my dark quarters will feel; but I am arrested by the Governor's voice. 'You, remain where you are. I shall require a witness.' Price laughs. I imagine he laughs at the absurdity of my being seriously considered a potential witness. It is not a guffaw or a snort, but a deep belly laugh that offends me. I am now determined to tell the truth, knowing that Price has not instructed me to be in any way devious; my deviousness will be my strict veracity to the facts. The Governor asks Price about the purpose of the journey, and why he was not informed. Price's answers are superficial in content and insolent in tone. The Governor is a man possessed; he does not take his eyes from Price. Then he comes to the heart of the matter. He asks what Price intends to do with the girl, and Price laughs. When he catches his breath Price suggests, 'Share her with you, Governor, if you're interested.' The Governor boils over and orders Price to take the girl back to where she came from. Price laughs on. The Governor, his voice now desperate, asks if it is Price's desire to completely undermine his authority. Price stops laughing. 'We stand,' says Price, 'at the edge of the world. The rules that bind normal men have no place in this land.' The Governor inches forward and tries to interrupt, but Price ignores him and continues. 'Here rank has little to do with privilege of birth – it is a matter of your ability to lead men and instil in them some respect for your position. Now who is here to strip off my epaulettes? Who to demote me? Who will back up your complaints? There is no superior officer for you to report me to, no society to sneer and point a finger at me for we are society, we men inside this Fort, and if I return to your world of silks and fine wines there you might reproach me, but here sweating in this hellish climate with these savages there comes a point at which your rank and order must fall away and be replaced by natural order. Do you understand me?' Price does not wait for an answer. He turns and walks slowly in the direction of his quarters. His jacket dangles from his hand and trails in the dirt. He has achieved his purpose and he saunters as though he imagines crowds parting in front of him. I look towards the weak Governor. At first I feared him for he seemed to want to take me in. Now I despise him because he lacks the ability to impose himself while still wishing to be considered worthy of leadership. The Governor turns and walks in the opposite direction to Price. I am abandoned.

Lewis restates his claim. 'Her screaming could have raised the dead. Damn near did for me,' he says. 'I thought she was a gonner.' He scratches at his sandy-coloured hair and continues. 'But then it seemed to go quieter, and then it started up again.' Lewis and I sit in our customary positions on the ramparts. The day begins to fade. 'While you were gone we saw the Governor all the time. Used to come and talk with us, trying to make hay while the sun shines if you know what I mean.' I do not know what he means but I listen. 'He's a rum sort. Can't get no understanding out of him at all. Still, he seems like the sort of fellow who might do you a good turn if you ever got in a spot of bother.' And so our conversation drifts on until Lewis once more hits upon his source of grief. 'But I can't believe they're leaving me behind. I came out here for some action, not to sit around while the others go out and enjoy themselves.' I try again to suggest to him that enjoying oneself plays little part in an expedition, but he does not listen to me. Cocooned as he is in his own misery I think it best to leave him alone. Once they have departed I will no doubt see and spend much time with him. By then I hope that he will have made peace with his situation which, when one examines it, is actually a blessing. I watch as young Lewis closes his eyes and drifts off to sleep. I stand and return to my quarters. Life is becoming predictable. These days I find myself desperate for the expedition to commence in the hope that there might be some change to this irksome daily pattern.

The rude shriek cuts through the night. Then silence. Then another scream. Then again silence. Then, at an irregular interval, yet another scream. It is the irregularity of the event that gives it such a haunting quality. One cannot prepare oneself for the irregular. I walk out into the night and wait. Again the scream. Will nobody go to her aid? I slump to the ground, my back propped up against the cold stone wall, and wait as though half-expecting my name to come singing out, a signal for me to charge into action. But I am not summoned. I am merely tormented by the endless cries of pain. The sun rises in the east.

I stand before Price. I am in his quarters. The girl is in the corner of the room, her body clearly (even from this distance) marked with what appear to be small blisters. Price seems anxious, his face creased with tiredness, his clothes crumpled as though he has not removed them for the last two days and two nights. 'I want you to take her back to where she comes from, I

32

have no further use for her.' I look at the girl. I wonder what she feels, if the inner person is as battered as the outer, but she reveals nothing. I imagine she is in pain, but the degree of hurt is well-concealed. 'Take the girl back and then return here as soon as possible,' I nod. 'Do you wish me to leave this instant?' Price, his face heavy with fatigue, looks up at me. 'There are two horses waiting in the courtyard. You must leave immediately.' Questions rattle around my head. Am I expected to spend the night with these people, for I cannot make the journey there and back in one day. But if I stay with these people there is a real danger that my life will come under threat for I have no illusions about my popularity. The look on Price's face dispels my notion of questioning him further. He will have nothing to say concerning matters of my comfort or safety. I turn to the girl and tell her that we must leave now. She stands and walks towards me. To my horror I see now the full extent of this blister-sketching on her body. She must be in considerable pain for some of these marks still run with pus. On her bottom lip there are incisions where she must have bitten hard to try and maintain consciousness during this violation. I say nothing further. I lead her out and down the steps and into the courtyard. She shields her eyes from the brightness of the day. I judge it best to remain silent until we are far away from the Fort. A soldier presents us with the horses. The girl is so weak that she cannot mount her horse with the same degree of independent panache that she possessed only two days previously. She places her bare foot into the cup of my hands and I hoist her up and on to the animal's back. We turn towards the gate and ride out of the Fort and back in the direction of her village. It is a return journey that I feel sure neither of us imagined would be so suddenly thrust upon us.

She rides on beside me refusing to answer my questions. I feel uncomfortable conversing in our native tongue, but I am sure that she understands me. 'What did he do to you?' Again she ignores me. She has heard my question, or has she? I wonder if something has happened to her hearing, but this cannot be.

She knew when to get up in Price's quarters. I look at this serene and beautiful girl and feel myself stiffening. It is many months since I have had a woman and there is nothing to stop me throwing this girl to the ground and spending myself inside her body. I am sure that she expects me to behave in this way. I begin to weigh up the reasons why I should not perform in such a manner. I finally decide that to take her can do little harm to my reputation with either camp. I lead my horse to the left and instruct her to follow. 'We will rest here for a while.' I reach up and help her down. She is frail, her waist narrow (that of a girl), her body limp. I sit next to her and drink. Then I pass the gourd and she drinks delicately and in silence. I pick a flower and begin to strip it petal by petal. 'So you will not tell me what happened to you?' I find myself speaking with a slightly threatening swagger, but I am unable to reverse into humility. She does not answer. 'He abused you physically but did he enter your body?' She stares out into open space. I reach over and touch her hand. 'Tell me, it is important.' She pulls away her hand and turns to look at me. Her deep brown eyes are brimmed with tears. Then one washes over and makes a river between the eye and the corner of her mouth. I trace its progress and feel ashamed of my concupiscence. 'Let us go,' I say. I stand up. It is only now that I notice the dampness on my thighs where I have been unable to control myself. I turn and walk some distance from her. I take out my manhood and charge a burnt-sienna arc on to the dusty soil. The viscosity that clings to the tip of my manhood confirms my indiscretion, but I feel a sense of relief and relaxation, although I do not recall the actual moment of ecstasy. It is a lost pleasure, but I am grateful to the girl. I put myself away and hope that somehow I might form a more permanent bond with this girl. I am no longer merely curious about her relationship with Price, or simply desirous of disgorging myself upon her. There is something more. She has a spirit that I have never before encountered. We ride on and I think of ways in which I might interest but not frighten her. I can think of none.

Smoke spirals from smouldering woodpiles that lie on this

worldly side of the protective bamboo fence. Perhaps these fires are intended to discourage evil spirits of the night. A dog that is little more than ribs dressed in thriftily stretched skin trots out to greet us. Its head remains low even when looking at us. A thin grey film is painted across both eyes and I realize the dog is blind. I turn to the girl for some sign that might bring us together. After all, I have done as I promised and brought her safely back home; I feel perhaps I deserve some kind of recognition for this, but she is not about to thank me. She harbours a boldness of spirit that were it lodged in anybody else would invite contempt. We enter her village. She rides ahead and her people come out to greet her. Nobody speaks. Her physical appearance shocks them. The Head Man appears. He looks from the girl to me, and then back again to her. She remains astride the horse and the Head Man eventually looks again at me. 'Is there anything else?' I shake my head. I want to establish that I am in no way to blame for the condition that the girl is being returned in, but I know that it will be better for everybody if I simply depart. The girl dismounts. I gather in the reins and turn. Despite the fact that it will soon be night they have not offered me accommodation. I ride, as slowly as dignity will permit, out of the village and back towards the darkness of the plains. I turn and see the new ribbons of smoke. I imagine they are preparing a feast and I hope that she is now happy. I have a long and difficult journey ahead.

I hear the noise of horses gathering in the courtyard. There is great shouting and much preparation for the expedition. I can visualize every last detail of the mobilization, so familiar am I with the whole process, but I feel that I ought to leave my quarters in case there is something new. I am the veteran of the Fort. I have participated in two dozen such expeditions. Now, for only the second time, they intend to leave me behind. There is a murmur that the trade may soon be ended. They have become desperate; there is little time for the preliminary duping of kings with lead bars in exchange for wooden masks and ivory statuettes. In fact, there is little time for trade, in the pure sense. Some goods are exchanged for corn, yams, plantains, and coconuts (which provide sustenance), but the human cargo is simply plundered. These days the soldiers have to travel further into the country. It is easy to underestimate the amount of preparation. To begin with we were away for days at a time, then it became weeks; the last expedition took over a month. I step into the light. The Governor and Price stand together as though making a show of their intimacy. They will ride out and leave the Fort in the charge of a man named Sturrock. But such a charge hardly taxes a man. Keeping discipline among half-a-dozen sun-dazed soldiers is not a demanding occupation. In reality Sturrock's only task is to make sure that the supply of rum and beer is not exhausted. I sit in the shade and wait for the trumpets to sound and the gates to be thrown open. Across the courtyard Lewis stands alone. He is a boy pining to be part of an adventure that is passing him by. A sad story is written upon his face. I want to go across and tell him to grow up, to be a man, but it is not my place to do so. And then the trumpets sound and the Governor's waiting is over. The more seasoned men whisper private prayers. They address their Gods.

Six men, plus myself, in a Fort of this size. It is a strange experience. There is such excess of space that it is possible to wander for hours without happening upon another soul. And when one does they are likely to be curled up in some corner, or staring out over the sea and moving only to swat insects. There is a new air of freedom, a luxury about the place. I devise a hobby spotting and naming the birds who live on the seaward side of the Fort. To this end I spend many whole days looking and mentally recording, but it is as futile an occupation as my previous attempts to ward off boredom. These have included trying to read a book in their language; as far as I could discern it simply related the various prices of grain and other trading materials in their unprocessed state. Not a particularly interesting book, and one not designed to encourage a person to pursue the art (for that is what they call it) of reading. I have also tried to interest myself in exercise, lifting heavy stones in a belated attempt to develop a physique, but I find such practice laborious and near-cousin to vanity. So I idle and pass day after day without conversation. I am keen to avoid the increasingly lugubrious Lewis who seems to have taken excessively to the bottle. I caught Sturrock lecturing him. Lewis appeared to be too drunk to digest the words. The one constant on my mind is the girl. Every time I recall her young limbs I am grateful to her for her part in enabling me to perfect a technique of thinking myself, without the aid of tactile stimulus, to the point where I can gain sexual satisfaction. She has proved herself a rare find in terms of helping me to sublimate the serious problem of my urges, but I find difficulty in holding her as an idea, knowing as I do that she is only a matter of a day's ride away. I keep throwing back my mind to the time when we stopped under the tree and I discovered the dampness on my thighs. I wish I had not suffered a surfeit of good taste and had gone ahead and taken her there, for at least the memory of such a conquest could have helped ease me through the nights that are at present proving such a torment. When the expedition returns it will be possible for me to sate my appetite in secret, in fact satiate it well beyond the normal capacity of a man of my years. I generally have so much stored energy that I am able to perform like an old bull for hours on end. But it is not simply a matter of sexual energy when I think of the girl. There is also the question of wanting to know what happened between her and Price. After all, he has never before lost control and had to seek out a woman in between the expeditions. I assume that, like everyone else, he has suffered in silence with his dreams and fantasies, although it has been suggested that he occasionally sodomizes the younger soldiers, a practice so common that it casts no adverse light on his masculinity in the eyes of anybody except the religiously trammelled. But what exactly did Price do to her, for clearly he exceeded the normally understood forms of gratification. The girl will be able to tell me not only about Price, but also about herself. And myself. What is it that I have lost that she has somehow managed to retain?

I cross the courtyard. There are no sentinels. I enter the stables

37

and take a horse that is mercifully quiet. I lead the nag out through the main gate, which is both heavy to open and heavy to swing back into place. I decide that once clear of the Fort I will ride as hard as possible, using the stars and moon as my guide. I aim to arrive in the morning so that if I am greeted with an immediate rejection I will be able to leave and return again under the cover of night. As the dark shadow of the Fort fades from view my only worry is that they will miss the horse. They are fed every day, but it is a risk I will have to take. I ride on but the worry is increasingly difficult to banish; it is clear that I will have to return. As dawn breaks I push open the gate and lead the horse across the courtyard and back into the stables. I retire to my quarters burdened with disappointment, defeated by my own wilful haste.

I sleep in daylight hours and wake at night. The pattern is reinforced over four days until I feel comfortable with the arrangement. I cannot get the girl out of my head. I determine that if I carry with me enough supplies, and keep close to waterholes, I can probably walk the distance to the village in two days and two nights. I know it is a foolish plan but what am I to do? Inside of me the idea has already burst.

Night falls and I am awake. I carry with me a stout gourd of water and some cornmeal that I have pilfered from the kitchens. I am ready. The first night is difficult, for the moon is not full and the howling of hyenas plays on my nerves. And then the sun comes up and I am tired, and the heat saps what little strength I have left in my body. I begin to slow until I finally collapse beneath a wild avocado tree. I open my gourd of water. Cows stand and look on. There are few farmers left. Wandering alone with their animals they are easy prey. The day is still and begins to spin. I wonder if it was not worth taking a chance on a horse. Perhaps I should have released all of the horses. The fact that one was missing would not have been an issue. But it is too late now. I must get to my feet and continue, but my body rebels. I lie prostrate on the parched earth. I open my eyes and see that the sun has set and I have lost valuable time. I am tempted to go back, but I get to my feet and walk on. The night is eerie and I feel tired and cold. I walk through the night consumed with a sense of fear, concerned that I should not stop. But as dawn arrives (and the heat begins to descend and then rise) I sit and rest under a tree. It is thirst that arouses me; I reach for my gourd and drain what little water remains out and into my mouth. Unless I chance across a waterhole I will now have to execute the rest of the journey in one broad effort. It is with this in mind that I step out. I realize I am in danger of failure. I fall to my knees, half in prayer, half in despair. I pitch forward on to my stomach and decide to sleep in this position in the hope that the morning sun will not burn my face. I wish to preserve my senses. I pull a cloth up and over my head.

I am not sure whether I am under the cloth. There is cloth all around me. I realize it is cloth in the form of bandages. My body is badly burned and bruised, but it has been treated with these bandages and oils. I see that I am in the same hut that Price slept in. Cured goatskins hang from the walls. Eventually they will be stretched over wooden frames and become drumskins. I stare at my dry and calloused feet. In the corner of the hut stand baskets of grain. I have no idea by what route, or by what wizardry I come to be here. I tongue my cracked lips and realize that I must find answers. I try to move but it is clear that I am an invalid. Not only can I not move, but I am too weak to shout. I lower my head back down and wait. I cannot bring myself to think of what it is they might have in store for me. There is little point to speculation. What will happen will happen. I need to rest. I close my eyes and try to encourage my mind to escape into a pleasant reverie of its own creation. But this is not possible.

I have lost the sense of time. By my elbow sits an untouched bowl of boiled rice and stewed yams. The smell turns my stomach. In the distance I hear somebody pounding a pestle. The Elder who spat in my face towers over me. He asks if I can stand. I try, but my body will not respond. He asks me to wait, but I have no means of going anywhere. He returns accompanied by the Head Man, who seems untroubled. I had imagined a fate much worse than the politeness with which I am being treated. They ask if it is really true that I walked from the coast. I answer them, but I am mystified that they do not ask why I have returned. It is possible that they have already assumed I have come back for the girl. But then it strikes me that I have no plan as to how I might encourage her to partner me, if indeed they will allow such a thing. The Head Man looks at me as though I am a wounded animal to be pitied. 'You will not be able to begin your return journey for two or three days.' I peer quizzically at him. 'We found you near to the village. A party of women had already noted your approach. It was only when you did not arrive at the expected hour that we sent out for you. But now you are here.' I try to look grateful, but the question of the girl keeps swirling around my head; I decide it is better to bring up the subject rather than continue to torment myself. I ask after her but they ignore my question. I know they heard me for a quick glance passed between them. I decide to force the issue. 'Is it possible for me to see the girl? I would like very much to see her.' Again they say nothing. 'Is it your purpose,' I ask, thinking now of the harsh nature of the journey I have made, 'to avoid all conversation about the girl, or is there something else that you wish to say to me?' They look at each other; eventually the Head Man speaks. 'It is not a pleasant matter. The girl has been ruined. She is no longer of us.' I feel a chill course through my body. 'Is she dead?' I ask. I now wish to circumvent any possibility of our misunderstanding one another. 'No, she is not dead.' The Head Man continues. 'Tomorrow, if you are able, we will accompany you to her. Until then you must rest.' They take their leave. I ponder on the girl, and I think of all the girls I have known, and again question why this one? I feel drowsiness enveloping my deliberations. My fatigued body is desperate for sleep; the journey to this village has exhausted what little energy I possessed; I am no longer a young man.

The Head Man and the Elder, plus two others of their generation, sit before me. Their combined persons now obscure the light that streamed in and made this hospital-prison tolerable. 'We want to ask you about the men with whom you live, and if they take our people to their deaths?' The Head Man speaks firmly. I do not know where to begin or what to say. I think I ought to try and stand or sit even, just to demonstrate that I am not completely helpless. I attempt to sit up, but it is not possible. I try hard to disguise the effort that I am spending, but they notice. I know now that I will not see the girl today. I resign myself to answering their questions and hope that I will not arouse their indignation. 'You see,' I begin, 'in many ways the man is just like us, except that he has certain technical skills in fire-power which place us at a disadvantage. However, we have a tendency to argue among our own people, while they are always able to put aside such disputes when it involves the achieving of a common aim. But, in their souls, they are not a peaceful people.' I stop and close my eyes and hope that this will suffice. I know full well that I have omitted to answer the part of the question that relates to our final destination. Inevitably it is this same question that the Head Man repeats, this time with increased vigour. I open my eyes. 'You have to understand that I know only what they tell me. I am led to believe that they take our people to their country to work for them in their fields; to harvest their crops in servitude, a servitude that they can rescue themselves from, but it is rare. As to the manner in which our people are treated, I cannot tell you for there are innumerable tales, some more palatable than others.' The men look at each other and whisper among themselves so that it is not possible for me to hear what they are saying. Then they make ready to ask me a further question, obviously one that they have arrived at by communal dis- cussion. 'Have you,' asks the Head Man, 'met any of our people who have been to their country and returned?' A look of worry creases my face. I try to wipe it off even as it appears, fearful that it will be misinterpreted. The implication behind the question is transparently obvious; they are anxious to know what has happened to their relatives and friends; they are eager to establish that they have not been automatically sacrificed to alien Gods. I can say nothing truthful that will alleviate their worry so I remain mute. They begin to talk among themselves. They stand up, and all but the familiar Elder leaves. He waits until the others have passed from view, and the hut has become brighter. He tells me that the meeting has been 'good' and they are satisfied with my answers to their questions. I watch this man, who cannot disguise his contempt for me. He stares back and announces that tomorrow morning the girl will be brought to me and that I am to take her and leave the village. I protest. 'But what if she will not come with me?' I explain that I cannot force her to leave, that she may wish to stay. 'There is,' begins the Elder, 'little chance that she will wish to stay. You must take her and never return or you shall both lose your lives.' There is no room for discussion; the words have been dealt with authority.

She crouches at my feet like a dog. Thinner now, and with permanent blotches where the burn-marks were, she stares at me with wide open eyes as though she has passed through a greater trauma since her return from the Fort. I feel sorry for her as a good measure of the lofty spirit seems to have been drained from her; this newly vulnerable character does not correspond to the person I am familiar with. I look beyond her and out of the hut. The darkness of night is being brushed by the first hints of a new day. With some difficulty I lean forward into a sitting-up position; I ask her if she will help me. She reaches out a hand and I touch her; a warmth flushes through my body. She holds my arm and hauls me to my unsteady feet as though equally determined to leave this village. A terrifying fear born of humiliation is written across her face; it disappoints me. I preferred the old humour. Like two thieves we stumble out of the hut. I notice that she has already refilled my gourd, and that she has with her supplies of dried meat and fruit. I lean slightly against her until I regain familiarity with the use of my legs. We leave and try to establish as much distance as possible between ourselves and the village before dawn breaks. The sun begins her daily onslaught on my body and I can walk no further. I have to sit down and rest in the shade of a weather-stripped tree. I am too debilitated to attempt conversation, but she does not seem to expect this. She rips pieces of cloth and binds them to my feet. I look at her and wonder if it concerns her that I am taking her back to the Fort; perhaps she does not yet realize this. I rest. The girl looks after me. There is a weak storm-light which blackens the sky and makes shadowy the outline of the distant bush. Two days and two nights pass. As the Fort comes into view I have a sudden rush of panic in case the expedition has been forced to return early. This would almost certainly seal our fate; but the flags are not flying. I suggest to the girl that we wait until nightfall before making our entrance. She nods. Still she has said nothing to me. We sit and rest under a bush. I notice the hasty passage of the clouds. As the wind rises trees bend slightly to let her pass. I look at the girl. Now that our goal is in sight I explain that she will be with me and not with the man who previously abused her. Again she nods. When she first did so I read this nodding as a sign of a major breakthrough. Now I merely see it as further evidence of her stubborn taciturnity. 'So tell me,' I ask, 'why is it that you will not talk with me?' She turns her face away and stares in the direction from which we have come. Then she looks back at me and opens her mouth, her lips clinging together until the last possible moment, and then she hovers. And then she simply lowers her head having changed her mind. She will not talk with me, but I know that it is only a matter of time before she finds the courage to do so. And so I wait, and we wait and stare at the massive outline of the Fort, and listen to the coarse whisper of the sea.

Perhaps the soldiers are beginning to notice that I am consuming more food than is normal. I do not mind so long as they do not suspect the real reason behind my excessive appetite. But then again, how could they? I take few chances. She comes out only at night for a breath of fresh air; the rest of the time she spends in my quarters. I bring her water and food; I attend to her needs and talk with her. And, of course, I make love to her, although I find this side of our relationship problematic for I associate our love-play with guilt. I worry that perhaps I

43

undertake such risks for mere physical gratification. I worry that she feels this, but we do not speak of it. I break a crust of bread and give the larger piece to her. 'Your father is the Head Man in your village?' I repeat the information, unable to believe that he could have treated his own daughter in this way. She looks at me and shrugs. 'As soon as the man chose me I was tainted. My father had to disown me. Have you already forgotten the ways of your own people?' I take the rebuke with a straight face, for in it there is an element of truth. There are many things about our people that I have forgotten. She causes me to remember. 'And it was only a matter of chance that he chose you on the day you lined up with the others?' She laughs. 'Of course it was chance. Do you think I wanted to go from my family into the arms of such a man? As he pointed towards me my life was over.' She stops. 'But you did nothing to help me and I hated you for that.' I feel I have to explain. I stand and walk away from her. She lies on the bed of straw. She has encouraged my wounds to heal and once again I feel whole. I walk with conviction. She would have made an outstanding wife for any man in her village, but I am forgetting that there are no eligible men in her village or in any village like hers. Women are one fifth the value of men. They are merely snatched to make up numbers if too many men die on the march back to the coast. 'I could do nothing to help you.' Even as the words fall from my mouth I know that they are the very words she expected to hear. 'You see I have no excuses for my present circumstances, they were thrust upon me and I accepted them. Some years ago a king's trader captured me and sold me to one of their factors. He, in turn, taught me the principles of their language and methods of trading. He seemed loath to allow me to join the coffle, partly on account of my age but also because, as he declared, he could espy some spark of intelligence. When he died (of his addiction to liquor and hot women) I was brought by his under-trading officer to this Fort and subjected to vile abuses until they realized that a replacement factor would not be forthcoming. I subsequently acquired some status in their eyes and began to assist them in their trading. But now their mode of trading has changed, and civilized gifts are not being proffered, permission to trade in restricted domains not being sought; there are no longer any meetings to interpret and my status has once more fallen off. My soul is not at peace. I sometimes wonder why I do not go with the rest of our people, but I fear what you fear, and what we all fear, that there may be awful misery beyond these shores.' I pause. 'I could not help you because I was frightened.' She stares blankly at me and I am unable to tell whether or not she believes a word of what I have just related. She asks me why, if I am so consumed with fear, I risk my situation by bringing her back here. There is much in this question that I cannot answer, but I present her with the simplest explanation. 'You see, I wanted to know what happened between you and Price, for that is the name of the man who came with me on the first journey. What did he do to make you scream? It appears to me as though he took a light and burned small patches of your skin. Is it this that made you scream?' She looks directly at me and does not hesitate with her answer. 'Well, it is this,' she says, 'and more. Yes, he burned me with fire, but he also entered me at the smaller end. Is this something that gives these people pleasure? He seldom spoke with me. For each mark of fire that he made on my body he entered me again but he never seemed to break into satisfaction, do you understand?' I nod, scarcely able to believe what I am hearing. 'And then my mouth, he took pleasure there, but again he could not break into satisfaction and I found it as painful but even more shameful for I could not scream. When he did not like the noise that I would sometimes make when he took pleasure at the back end, he would use my mouth to quieten me and say that if he felt my teeth he would kill me.' 'He did this?' Could Price not see that this is a beautiful and sensitive sixteen-year-old girl, not some whore to whom a broken piece of mirror glass will suffice to purchase any amount of degradation? Maybe he has forgotten the difference, if ever he knew there to be one. I have to control my feelings of anger. 'And did you tell your father of these incidents?' She smiles, her white teeth perfectly uniform in brightness and spacing. 'Of course I did not tell my father. He is a man. In our tradition he is able to give up a daughter more readily than he would his pride or his position in the village. When I returned they asked nothing of me, having already decided that I was unclean. Perhaps they thought my presence would poison others.' The girl tries to remain jovial but it is a simple matter to detect her pain. 'I was sent to a hut on the far side of the village, out of sight and sound of everybody else. I was expected to manage by myself.' She laughs and I encourage her to keep her voice down. 'You see,' she says, this time in a whisper, 'I would almost certainly have died if you had not returned. I have no experience of looking after myself, unlike others who are taught from an early age the use of the spear, shield, and hoe. I was the Head Man's daughter, I had no reason to acquire the skills of hunting or cultivation.' I wonder if her general tone is meant to offer up evidence of how grateful she is to me. 'Is there something else you wish to ask?' I sit next to her and take her hand. I hope that she will not resist. She does not. 'There is nothing further I have to ask of you,' she says. 'I have asked questions and you have given me your answers. I do not think that we should exhaust each other with questions that merely repeat what it is that we both already know.' Her wisdom surprises me. I turn my head towards her and kiss her on the mouth. She does not respond but I am keen to explore what I have now tasted. I push her back and lie beside her on the straw. Then I tease one hand around behind her head and kiss her again, and this time her lips are slightly moist and parted, ready to receive me. She entwines me in her arms and legs and I mount and enter her in the right place and deposit myself quickly. She caresses me and makes me feel as though our love-making has been prolonged and exhausting. She falls asleep in my arms. It has often occurred to me that I might have forfeited the right to the emotion of love by virtue of my present situation. I know now that this is not the case. That I can care, that I have the capacity to touch and feel tender, to look after a small child (although she hates me calling her this), shocks me, but makes it possible for me to rediscover some form of self-respect. I shall stop worrying about who might have noticed that the supplies are low, although I will still exercise a caution that is bred of habit. There remains but one worry; the return of the expedition. Their reappearance will make my life more complex, for while it is possible to disguise the presence of the girl with six others present, the return of the expeditionary force will herald the start of my work and the introduction of much vigilance around the Fort. I begin to think about running away with the girl.

The call of the trumpet wakes us simultaneously. I feel a sudden wave of fear pass through me. I had not bargained on their arriving back so soon. I look at the girl who is startled. I say nothing in case I frighten her any more than is necessary. Again the trumpet sounds and I hear the noise of hooves in the courtyard and the shouting of men relieved to be back on the coast. 'Just wait a moment.' I get up and go to the door. I look out and guess that it must be near dawn. We have reached that part of the year when there is a chill in the air, when it is not possible to sit out all night under the moonlight. The night bites. I notice that some of the soldiers have wrapped scarves around their mouths and wear their collars turned up. But there are only five soldiers. I am not seeing the whole group, merely the advance party. I wonder if there has been an accident? Certainly the noises they are making suggest that something has gone wrong. This is no ordinary return; and they have arrived without captives. I am confused and retreat back into the room. I lie down next to the warm body of the girl and assure her that there is nothing to worry about. She seems to accept this and closes her eyes. She turns over on her mat and is soon asleep; she breathes deeply and peacefully.

The noise dies down and I decide to venture forth in an attempt to search out the root of this mystery. I walk close to the walls of the Fort for I would prefer to pass undetected. And then I see him, the one whom I know will tolerate a short conversation with me. Lewis is drunk, in much the same state as he was when I last saw him. Unruly stumps of hair sprout from his scalp. I cannot help but think of this apparition as a waste of a young man; he is perishing on this coast and will probably never find his way back to the arms of his people (if indeed he has people). Were he to return he would do so as merely a shell of the young boy who went away. I call to him and suggest that he comes down from the ramparts so that we might talk. He waves and beckons me up to him. A foolish smile spans his face; he is unable to disguise the fact that he is delighted to see me. I wonder if he has been ostracized. Nobody can tolerate a drunk for long, particularly a young drunk. We live in a closed and unforgiving society. I look around and ensure that there is nobody else in sight. (I imagine the returnees have now settled down to their day's rest before making a full report to Sturrock.) I climb up to the ramparts and stretch out a hand which Lewis pumps lustily. 'You've been avoiding me,' begins Lewis, his voice slipping and slurring over the words. 'You think there's something wrong with me, is that it?' I muster a friendly laugh and pat him on the back. 'No, of course there's nothing wrong with you. I've been thinking and trying to wade through the debris of my life. That's one of the fine things about an empty fort, you're able to think for yourself without any pressure.' Lewis laughs. 'I'm not like you, always thinking, thinking. I've got other things to do.' I nod. 'Well, now that they're back we all have other things to do.' Lewis takes the bottle from his mouth. 'They're not back, only a few of 'em came back with the Governor. He's sick; struggling bad. Apparently the jungle and such was too much for his old body so Price told them to cart him back to the coast for some rest. They had to support him on horseback, a man on either side propping him upright. Looked real strange, like the Governor had given up the ghost, but I reckon he's got too much pride to die.' Lewis laughs, then takes a huge swig and offers me the bottle. I smile and vaguely wave my hand. I try not to mark my face with the revulsion that I feel. 'I can tell,' says Lewis, 'that you're not a drinking fellar. Never mind, you'll some day learn how to sup like a man. Did they never offer it to you before?' I look at young Lewis and throw my mind back to when I first arrived at the Fort. For some reason they felt it appropriate to make me dance and sing and drink alcohol until my body could no longer function normally. I kept falling over and then picking myself up again, and then the yellow-green fluid began to come up from my stomach and out through my mouth and I vowed that never again would I touch this alcohol that made a pig of men. It is an evil brew that holds no fascination for me. 'No,' I say to Lewis, 'you must drink your drink for it is far too precious to share, although I appreciate the generosity of your gesture.' Lewis smiles a gappy grin, a tooth having fallen out since the last time I saw him. 'Well,' he asks, 'how long you reckon before the others arrive back?' 'Normally,' I say, 'it would be another two weeks or so.' Lewis nods. 'That's what the other soldiers said, reckoned they'd got some of the finest cargo; big, tough, and strong, difficult to ship, so they claim, but profitable once over the other side. Everybody seems in fine spirits except the Governor.' I realize now there are only two weeks before I will have to justify the girl's presence, or abscond. But all my thoughts of defection charge into the same insurmountable truth: they will come to search me out. I hold too much knowledge about their ways and methods of operation; I speak their language. I am loath to admit defeat but it is difficult to imagine that I will be able to disguise the girl's presence indefinitely. Again I thank Lewis for the offer of a drink. I leave the ramparts and go back down to the court-yard and pass into my quarters. She is awake and sitting up waiting for me. 'I was frightened that something might have happened to you. What is happening out there?' I explain to her that an ailing Governor has returned with a handful of soldiers. The bulk will not be returning for a further two weeks. She falls silent, and then in a whisper she asks what is likely to befall us when all the men return. I run a hand through her wiry hair and cup her fat, puppyish cheeks in my palms. 'I don't know.' Her broad lips flicker and I push mine up against hers and squeeze my tongue through and into her mouth. She seems to find much solace in these moments of impromptu love-making. There is no exploitation, only shared fear and insecurity as we rock together. Her hand reaches down and guides me (she no longer expects me to find my own way) into her. Through familiarity we give each other the moment of pleasure at the same time. It eases tension. We separate and lay on our backs and stare at the stone ceiling. 'What kind of man is this Governor?' asks the girl. It is a good question. I remember him walking me round and round the courtyard and trying to wrestle from me the secret, if indeed there is such a thing, of life on the coast. I explain to her that he is a man who I have come to mistrust because of his weakness. Despite the brutish mentality of the man, I always feel more comfortable with Price. She listens in silence. And then she speaks: 'But can this Governor not help us?'

The door to his quarters is slightly ajar. A soldier sleeps near by. It is difficult to tell if this soldier is meant to be on guard duty; if so he is located too far away from the door. I enter. The Governor lies under a white mosquito net. His skin seems to have taken on a yellowish pallor and small rivulets of sweat decorate his temples. I wonder if he is in the grip of a fever. As though aware that somebody is with him in the room, his eyes open and he stares up at me without the slightest degree of alarm. 'So,' he begins, 'are you really come to visit, or are you come here to do harm to an old man who lies stricken in his bed?' I take a step forward. 'I am here to visit. I am curious as to your condition.' With some difficulty the Governor props himself up and then gestures to me that I should close the door so that we might talk with more privacy. I cross the room and close the door. When I return he points to the end of the bed and I sit and wait for him to speak. 'I need somebody to read to me. You do read, don't you?' I nod. 'And write too?' I nod again. 'Good,' says the Governor, 'I need somebody to read to me from the Bible. Do you know the Bible?' I shake my head. From underneath the pillow he pulls a beautiful leather-bound book. 'It contains the story of our God and all the wisdom of our people.' He offers up the book and I take and finger it. I am fascinated by the possibility of glimpsing into the world of their Gods. I can see that the book has been well-used by many generations. Despite its age there is little dust that clings to it; a great deal of love and attention has been lavished on this particular volume. I put it down and wonder what I am supposed to do. He watches me closely then encourages me to pick it up again and read to him a few lines. I open the book

50

somewhere near the middle and begin to read. He closes his eyes as though in ecstasy. And then I stop. I understand the words but not the context; the power of these words eludes me, and it frightens me that somebody should be so moved by my reading of passages that I do not understand. Before I proceed any further I would like to know more. I try to frame a question. 'Are you happy?' asks the Governor. 'Do you feel peace in your heart?' He opens his eyes. They seem to me stupid questions to ask somebody who is being held captive, but the absurdity does not seem to have penetrated the mind of the Governor. 'You see,' he goes on, 'I ask you this for I have now met your people in their feral state, many of them, and their near state of perfect nakedness, their baseness of tongue, and ignorance of Christianity makes it reasonably obvious that they can never be happy until they have digested some of the basic lessons of our civilization. But you are a mystery; you seem to have some of the benefits of our ways but still you are not, I do not think, happy. I wonder, do you imagine this lack of happiness relates to our dwelling here on this coast?' 'Perhaps,' I say. The Governor sighs. I continue. 'These are not pleasant times for any of us, whatever our language or our customs; whatever our religion or our beliefs.' The Governor looks at me. 'I fear you may be correct,' he says. 'I fear the wheel of history has spun us all into a difficult situation, and no amount of acclimatizing by you or by me is going to heal the wound that this economic necessity has inflicted upon our human souls.' He pauses for a moment. 'But your people, it is possible you may never recover from this intrusion. I am led to believe that certain chiefs have been known to raid their own villages and seize people of customs, language, and manners near to their own, then subject them to the whims of factors in exchange for brandy. Imagine being able to pay a king or a chief in alcohol to round up his own people and reduce them to little more than horses tied to posts. Is it any wonder that there is some debate as to whether you have in you the capacity for reason? Bells, baubles, bars of lead, beer, such things sway the minds of your so-called leaders and they willingly aid in this business. These days we no longer deem you worthy trading partners, we just pillage. It is confusing for,

51

as I have already maintained, there is potential in the evidence of yourself.' The Governor coughs. 'Do you see me as a man? Do you see me as your superior? I am curious.' He lurches as another cough rattles through his body. 'I would like to know how you view me.' I realize there is little point in trying to construct a disingenuous answer. The Governor is distressed enough to want the best answer, in fact the only answer possible, so I decide that I will give it to him. 'You see,' I say, 'I think of you as a man, but a man with power which I suppose makes you my superior. I view you as a man who at present has some idea of how to dominate other men, but that is all.' He smiles and thanks me for my honesty. 'I think you have the capacity to be a statesman among your people. What was your former role?' He looks at me with a new respect. 'I was a shepherd,' I say, 'but being a shepherd is a respectable occupation. What you have to understand is that all occupations are respectable, but they bear little relationship to the status in which you are held by your own people.' Again he smiles at me. 'And you, I assume, were held in high status?' 'It is true. I was perhaps destined to one day become the Head Man.' The Governor is quiet. Then he speaks with his eyes lowered as though personally responsible for my demise. 'I am sorry.' He reaches out his hand for the Bible which I pass back to him. 'You are a man whom I would like to help.' My heart leaps. 'You see, it is only now that I have witnessed the abject barbarity of your savage people that I can fully appreciate the distance – the somewhat remarkable distance that you have travelled along the path of civilization. That you can read and write places you in a position of superiority over many people in this Fort. Do you realize what your achievements are, what they could mean for your people? I am astonished that it has not been suggested to you that you return to my country with one of the trading ships, for your presence there would go some way towards silencing the anti-trading lobby. If only they could see the evidence of Christian work in the shape of your person then I believe that some of the present difficulties would be eradicated; some of the hypocrisies would disappear overnight and you would soon find yourself fêted as a celebrity, does that not appeal to you in some way? Surely there must be some part of your soul that desires recognition?' I smile, not daring to reveal to this man that at present there is only one part of my soul that requires any kind of attention and that is the part that relates specifically to the girl. 'I would like you to come and visit me tomorrow. We must talk more,' he says, 'we must decide how best we might nurture your burgeoning fame.' I suspect the Governor will probably 'understand' the question of my love and see it as another example of how I have managed to raise myself up above the animal. I am tempted to ask him about his own feelings, and if he has left behind a wife and family, but I do not. It will wait. I stand and back out of the room. 'Until tomorrow,' I say. He looks at me with his large eyes, feeling that he has made a discovery, not realizing that for all his concern, for all his caring, he has not even asked after my name.

I find Lewis astride her, his manhood in her hand, an empty bottle of liquor on its side. He pushes the girl on to her back and one of her legs flies high in the air and then wraps itself neatly around his shoulders. She looks at me with wet liquor-sodden eyes. Lewis laughs. 'You crafty little bastard, keeping her here for yourself. You never took her anywhere, did you?' She smiles at Lewis and then cups her mouth around him and draws him in with a loud noise. 'She's like a bleeding machine. You can't satisfy a girl like this by yourself. You ought to be grateful that I found her.' At the moment of triumph (and failure) Lewis's face turns ugly and he begins to quake. 'My God!' he cries, 'Jesus Christ!' She lets him go and wipes the mess from her mouth with the back of her hand. 'Look,' says Lewis, 'you're not to let anyone else know. If anyone finds her then you're in for it. I'll just deny that I ever saw her, let alone tasted her.' I nod. I am barely able to control the anger that is coursing through my body. But towards whom is this anger directed? I suspect that it is directed towards myself. A sated Lewis puts himself away, picks up the empty bottle, and leaves. I stand before the girl. 'He came looking for you,' she says. Her mouth remains damp. 'I could not understand him, and I feared for you if I failed to attend to him.' I say nothing. It

53

terrifies me that she might have enjoyed giving satisfaction to Lewis. Perhaps she has the skills of a whore that enable her to give while remaining aloof from the receiving of pleasure. I ask her: 'Did you get satisfaction?' She lowers her eyes. 'Of course not.' I have little choice but to trust her for there are no means by which I might enter the emotional state of her mind or body. However, I suspect my feelings for her cannot survive having to again witness such debauchery. Similarly, I am not sure how I would react to Lewis were he to have the audacity to repeat his performance in my quarters. The boy has probably never before used the same woman twice. Tomorrow I will go straight to the Governor and parade my civilized love for a woman whom I wish to take for my wife. I will explain to him the origins of her present state, but in a fashion that will not appear overly censorious towards Price. I hope that by offering my continued service to the Fort there might be some way of making regular my irregular domestic arrangements.

I cannot touch her. She keeps me awake with her girlish sobbing. The image of Lewis astride her, and shuddering with the pleasure that she gave to him, is too much. I cannot feel even the slightest amount of stiffness. She reaches down hoping to induce some, but I spin away and offer her my back. Her distress grows in volume and I pray for the new day to arrive so that I might visit with the Governor.

I stand by the entrance to his room and stare at his rigid body. I am fearful of how I might act if I return to my quarters and find Lewis once again spending his seed. The Governor's death is a merely practical blow. I have seen much death and have come to look upon her as a warm and seductive friend who encourages one to take her hand and make a journey. Once in death's valley there is no anxiety; one merely wishes to lie down and fall into a deep sleep with neither worries nor fears. One draws one's own curtains. I turn from the body.

She still sobs, but at least she is alone. We stare at each other and I think it best to explain what has happened and hope that she will survive the magnitude of this blow. However, she re-doubles her weeping with such extravagance that I am forced to place my hands over her mouth. 'It is not the end of the world.' I hear my foolish voice. Then Lewis appears. He carries with him a piece of paper which he hands to me. It is folded double so I cannot read it. 'This is for you', he says. Then he runs his hand across the top of the girl's head. 'I miss her, but I've got some duties to take care of. Maybe later.' He turns on his heels and leaves. I open the letter but there is nothing on the paper. I put down the letter – if a letter is what it constitutes – regarding it as a stupid deceit. It is the first letter that I have ever received but there are no words. I accept it as Lewis's excuse to reappear with some guise of purpose in order that he might see the girl. For such as I, who only acquired the skills of writing and reading in their language by the application of much effort, it is a cruel joke.

Again Lewis laughs and mounts her roughly, his manhood projecting stiffly from his pants. He laughs all the time as though she is some toy that he has been given to play with. He does not seem to understand that she has feelings. Perhaps these men cannot think when their manhood is hard. I roll up my fists and avert my head. These past weeks I have endured the spectacle, unable to interrupt, frightened of what might happen to me should I do so. Have I finally lost control of my life? I squat by the slop pail knowing that the woman I suffer for, the woman I brought back to this Fort at great risk to my life, is being abused and I am powerless to help. Lewis steps back and tucks away his looseness, and I find my mind organizing the words. The girl buries her head in the dirty straw. 'Lewis,' I say. My grey years command little respect. I know that I am courting disaster. 'Lewis, I do not think you should come back here again.' Lewis looks puzzled. He cannot believe that I might be ordering him to do something. 'Is she diseased? Or is there something else you have not told me?' I can see the panic in his eyes. 'It is not that,' I say. Lewis scratches his head. 'Does she not want me to come again, is that it?' 'Yes, that is it,' I lie, 'she no longer wants you.' Lewis takes a step forward. 'But she wants you, right?' His voice is cut with jealousy. 'Or is it you who've told her to say this for you want her all for yourself?' I have to stand firm now for I am in danger of being humiliated by the vitriol of this man. 'You see,' I say, 'it is possible for her to have opinions of her own that are not injected into her head by me. And it is also possible for me to tell you that you are not welcome here any more. She is not meant to be taken like a whore.' He laughs in disbelief. 'And what if I were to report you for this? Well? You must have taken leave of your senses.' I know now that my fate is sealed but I try to maintain a façade. 'I have said all that I am able to say. I trust to your discretion. I cannot say any more than this.' Lewis snorts, then turns and marches from the room, and I feel healthier. Even though she is still damp from another man I go to her and tell her what I have just said and we hold each other. Why have I ensured my demise in this way? Perhaps I should have simply looked in the other direction.

I leave the girl and step out into the courtyard. The coffle has finally arrived with its noise and smell. The men, women, and children wear heavy wooden collars that are secured with iron rings and linked to the person in front and the person behind by means of a cumbrous chain. The soldiers eye their captives, rope whips poised, muskets cocked, and it is written clear and bold on their faces that this return march to the coast has left them near drained of energy. They will have walked through fields of tall grass, past villages freshly deserted save for the smoke that billows idly from straw roofs, along river banks (trying all the while to ignore the human shrieks of alarm that well up from behind the impenetrable curtain of forest that skirts the water); they will have followed the path of bleached bones that authenticates the trading trail. At the end of each day the soldiers will have handed the captives a small measure of grain and watched as they tried but failed to rest their heads on the ground. Those not on sentry duty will have found little sleep as all night the calls echo from hill to hill, crickets and tree-toads snap and croak, jackals bark, and then mercifully the cock crows for it is morning and the stifled sobs of the captives are only fully understood when the sun rises and illuminates their desolate faces, for they know that today they must again trudge with the dew on their bare feet and the wood and iron around their necks. The soldiers snap their whips and instruct the man at the head of the coffle to strike a steady drum beat to which the captives will march. And now they are returned. I wonder if Lewis has informed Price? I face both Price and the captives, but Price looks at me as though this is a routine sorting that we have to complete. They, of course, look upon me with astonishment, disturbed by the ease and fluency with which I speak this strange tongue. I admit to Price that some of their languages baffle me. It is a problem I have encountered with increasing frequency since the soldiers' adventuring began to draw them out and into more distant parts. Price frowns. 'But can you not speak with one of intelligence who might speak with others and in this manner form a bridge of communication?' I nod and begin, knowing that I am despised by my own for my treachery. This is surely the worst tragedy that can befall a man; but I am a survivor. It is a cold beginning, for normally I would have accompanied the soldiers and factors and assisted in their trading with the kings and chiefs. I would have already practised linguistic duplicity and, by observing the coffle, learned much about the captives. But times have changed and trading has become more desperate. My task is now simple: to help arrange the shackling of one man to another man of a different tribe and language or dialect, in order that difficulties of communication might further induce isolation and prevent the planning of communal rebellion. I must listen and act, and listen and report, and point out those who might destroy the imagined harmony of our commercial household. My first day's work is always the most trying as I begin to prise the fit from the weak, the liar from the honest man, the pregnant from the bloated, with no regard for status or familial connection: at the same time I attempt to block from my ears their taunting and threats. This sorting takes many days but there is no relief for it is eventually replaced by the agony of waiting for the ship to arrive, and being forced to listen to their low moaning, and enduring the awful wind-borne stench. Back in my quarters I sit with the girl and together we plan our escape. Once the cargo has sailed, and the sentinels have sunk back into the arms of lethargy, we two will hoist our masts and strike inland. I believe that despite my circumstances she loves me.

Price enters the room. He holds a handkerchief to his mouth. He looks at me and scowls. Behind him, and blocking the light from the door, stands Lewis. I wonder why it has taken him so long to betray me. But it is too late to ask. Price walks over to the girl and looks at her scarred body, much as a painter admires a canvas of his own creation. He turns and circles the room in a wide and ostentatious arc until he is in front of me. Then I watch him draw back his fist with slow deliberation. The contact numbs my face and knocks me to the ground. I do not feel pain, but blood fills my mouth as though it were saliva. The world shakes and then fades away to a misty silence.

I listen to the endless sighing of dying surf while mosquitoes feed on the open sores around my neck and ankles. It is too dark to see the faces of those next to me: I hear their voices, recognize various dialects, brush rats from my body on to theirs, and fight with them for my share of yam and coarse bananas. Two days ago the ship fired a cannon as a signal of its arrival. I imagined the unloading of bolts of colourful cloth, trinkets, blankets, rum, brandy and other strong water. I calmed my fellow captives by explaining to them the significance of the explosion and thereby revealed my identity. Movement is restricted (we are chained by the ankles and the neck), but those who could beat me did so with weary passion. Now they let me be. The air is stale, unfit for breathing, and carries loathsome smells that I know lead quickly to disease and death. I have too much time to think. There are steps, small and precise, that I have taken which have helped these intruders to subject thousands of my people to this abasement. It is too late to feel guilty, and there is nobody to whom I might realistically apologize. I do not feel like a traitor, I feel like a fool. I think of my village life, of women who carry children on their backs in cotton slings, of sleeping on bullock hides that lie across bamboo pallets, of dusty foot trails through wide valleys, of talking drums that echo through muddy creeks, of hacking at green wood with bush knives, of sweet wild berries, of voices raised in a death wail, of the girl. In this dungeon the musicians and holy men begin to sing, to feed the spirit with songs of hope. I assume the girl to be in with the women. I feel sure Price will have no further use for her. Here is darkness, sickness, waiting, men, dying, and song; but I have long since forgotten the words to their songs.

Fruit bats burst suddenly into the air as night begins to fall. A soldier, his mouth tight with concentration, mops the sweat from his brow and then turns the iron rod in the fire, dips the head in palm-oil to prevent it sticking, and burns the letters into the final neck and thigh. The boy does not scream, but the soldiers have to carry him by his arms and legs and place him back with us in the centre of the courtyard. He is momentarily too weak to walk. The ship rides at anchor and many have already boarded. When the wind rises it blows to me the smells of human misery: there is death in the air. The surgeon has examined this etiolated cargo for venereal taint, pliancy of limbs and joints, distemper, sore eyes, and done so without the least distinction of modesty. None are rejected for the trade is a game of chance. At this moment of transfer a chest full of small arms, ready-loaded and primed, is in sight. The soldiers are fearful. The sheer wretchedness of watching threatens to over-take their lives. They look on and pray that for them this trading intercourse might come to a swift and safe conclusion. There is liquor to be consumed. I look around and see Lewis, his face serene and bathed in torchlight. I wonder if his stubbled aspect is deliberate, a gesture of newly acquired manhood. Price stands with the new 'linguist', a young man who barks orders at us in our language and then turns and converses with them in theirs. I pity him. Under my breath I begin to mutter. Other lips move independently, and without organization we swell into a choir. I realize that this is the same choral chant that I would listen to when I was the man next to Price, the same hitherto baffling rebellious music that now makes a common sense for we are all saying the same thing; we are all promising to one day return, irrespective of what might happen to us in whatever land or lands we eventually travel to; we are promising ourselves that we will return to our people and reclaim the lives that are being snatched away from us. And the promise comes from deep inside of our souls, it comes from a region where it is impossible to pretend, it comes from the heart.

('Oyez! Oyez! Oyez! Freshly arrived on the trading ship, *Young Saint Paul*, I present to you the prime nigger heathens of the day. Praise be to the Lord!') I listen to this well-liveried man and understand what he says, but I have decided to feign ignorance of their language. I erase all expression, save that of fear. We survivors have been further divided. We have already said our goodbyes. As this happened I looked again for the girl but without success. My life is ended. ('Yours for life, for your son's life, and your son's sons's life') I am now resigned to the permanence of our separation. Neither my long-forgotten wife, nor my disregarded son, discovered a way to minister to my cold heart. The girl channelled an impossible route. ('A bargain! Who'll take this old woman? Let's call her "Venus". Take her! I'm in a festive mood.') It is my turn to promenade before the man and be prodded and jabbed. I step forward, after 'Venus' the least of the litter. ('Who'll make me an offer?') I stand on the platform and look down. I am an old man. The yoking together is over. My present has finally fractured; the past has fled over the horizon and out of sight.

II

The Cargo Rap

Dear Mother,

Today I celebrate (yeah 'celebrate' – remember they read this bull) my sixth year in captivity. But do not assume that you are all free. You are not. Most of you cannot see your chains. This is a serious error that some of us both inside and outside are fighting to correct. You do not see your chains, you do not hear them, but try leaping up the ladder a few rungs and you will sure as hell feel them.

Moma, you've spent most of your life working for some white woman in one house or another, and I will bet it has never crossed your mind that you might exchange places with her? I will tell you why you do not let it trouble your head. First, because the slave owners have led you to believe that you have a 'natural' position; in other words, under the heel of their boot. Darwin was an Englishman who formalized 'the law of the jungle' idea that you eats or you gets eaten. Claimed it to be a 'natural' law. Well Darwinism and Capitalism are kinfolks – they feed each other. It is only logical that two hundred years of exposure to the idea of a 'natural' (inferior) position should have nappied your mind. The second reason you never think you might want to exchange places with the rich white woman is because you're not stupid. You have a sense of self-preservation. You might not see or hear your chains, but you sure as hell can feel them cutting into your precious ebony skin. You know that if you leap you are going to get hurt so you just rest your slave butt up on your slave block and try not to think about these things.

Now, what some of us are trying to do is to set you free; to help you acknowledge and locate your chains, then we can give you the key to turn the lock so you can set yourself free. There's plenty of brothers out here preaching a tactile revolution. Your last letter caused me much sorrow. Let me address it.

You say you don't want anything to do with these 'trouble-makers'. That you assume black people to be the 'trouble-makers' is evidence of your slave mentality. The 'trouble-makers' are those who set dogs upon unarmed men and women, who shoot and bomb children in a church in our home town, who turn firehoses on black people to prevent them marching peaceably on the sidewalk. These people lynch, kill, terrorize, and maim our people and you call brothers 'trouble-makers'! These people are the inventors of the American sport of 'nigger-lynching'. Come a Saturday night Mr Charlie likes nothing better than to go out and crack a coon or two. Moma, Bull Connor ain't no Bull. He's a pig. The white man in a uniform with a big stick and a piece of death strapped to his hip is a pig, and pigs squeal and grunt when they see something badder than them and that's the law of the jungle.

Please send me a photograph of you and Pop. Did you forget to send one this Christmas? Maybe the pigs took it. 'Christ Mass'. It's funny how words get kind of shrunken up. Aunt Sophie came to visit with me. I know she's your sister, and I recognize that now they've moved me down here she is the closest to me geographically and all, but I told you before Moma I'd rather she didn't visit me. I'll amplify upon this in my next communication. Please send me a photograph of Laverne. When do you think it would be proper for me to start re-educating her? I take it you are aware that she is being malprogrammed in a hostile and alien culture? Look at me if you need evidence of this truth. But now I am rebuilding myself. Do you intend to deny me access to her mind until, as you put it, I reform my ways?

Ever,

Your son the 'trouble-maker'

Dear Pop,

I hear what you're saying but it's no part of my game plan to alienate Moma. Damn, she bore and birthed me, watched me wriggle out hot and sticky from between her legs, and witnessed the doctor cutting the cord through which she'd fed me when I was curled up inside of her and unable to hunt for myself. I repeat, I have no intention of alienating such a person. These ties are deep, ugly, bloody and real, however I must off-load what is on my (liberated) mind and share with both of you my perceptions of the world otherwise I am in danger of lying to you and, even worse, lying to myself.

When I said to Moma that I did not want her to send me a Christmas card with white people on it – in fact, I didn't want her to send me a Christmas card period – this was not meant to be taken as a personal insult. How could it possibly be so interpreted? Is Moma not a brown-skin woman? A black woman of African extraction? I was simply asking her not to waste hard-earned money peddling images of the enemy. And I meant it when I said it would be like sending me a K K K magazine.

I remember spending one summer as a fourteen-year-old down in southern Georgia with your brother, Uncle George, and Aunt Clytie. I remember you sent Laverne and I down there so you and Moma could get some peace and nurse Popa Williams and do whatever else it was you wanted to do once you got the two kids out of the way.

I used to love going down there and protecting my little sister all the way, arm draped around her tiny shoulders as the bus spluttered and shuddered through the night towards our destination. Then once we got there we would play outside with the animals, splash about in natural pools, and in the evenings I got to explore the cracks and crevices of the girls like you would a forest or woodland. But one morning Uncle George carried me into town and I saw the cowardly level to which the white man will sink. I did not blame the black child, but they had that boy selling KKK papers and nobody had the wind to go up and explain to him just what it was that he was doing. No, not even Uncle George. Well I don't want to receive any Christian cards through my mailbox, Popa, and if that disturbs Moma then let me hustle a favour from you; explain to her why. You're a man, you have the power to discipline your woman so use it!

You asked me so I will share with you a few words about my conditions. You seem to assume that I am in some way guilty of something, that my being here is the logical end result of my behaviour. Do I read you right? My conditions that you ask about are simple. I am a captive in a primitive capitalist state. I live on Max Row in a high-security barracoon. Forty-five per cent of my fellow captives are of the same colour as the captors. Fifty-five per cent of us – the wretched of the earth – are Africans. We live on the bottom level of this social swill bucket. I am at the very bottom. There is no parole from Max Row. First I have to get back into the main prison population. How do I achieve this? By drinking from the swill bucket.

Pop, I need some good woollen socks. I am cold. Please write clearly on the envelope what you are enclosing. Color, size, everything.

Later,

Rudy

Dear Pop,

I think about you a lot. About your rusty bruised hands. About your brow, always lined and furrowed. Have you stopped doing so much worrying? Thinking is better than worrying. It is a creative force which involves harnessing the energy you put into worrying and rechannelling it. It is a matter of discipline, but then so much of life concerns this one word, discipline.

You are a disciplined man. You always get up in the morning and drag your beat-up bones out to work, all kinds of weather, all kinds of white folks trying to kick on you, but still you get up and get out and get on because you know you got mouths to feed. I admire that about you. Neither Popa Williams, Laverne, me, nor Moma ever gone hungry because you were too lazy to discipline your body. Do you get what I'm working up to here? You see, I want you to start disciplining your mind. Only then can you be truly free and begin to impart to Moma and Laverne the truth about this plantation society. (I think Popa is too old to begin now. He's paid his dues many times over).

I have a routine which I want to share with you. I wake up at maybe 5 a.m. It is difficult to be precise about time because the light in my cell burns constantly. (To compensate for this I have developed the ability to tell time by the different noises that I hear in the corridors. There are different types of silence, some closer to dawn than others.) Then I exercise for two to three hours, slowly stretching all my limbs until they are sinewy and supple, then I hit the floor and pump out one thousand finger push-ups. Then more stretching. After this I study books, particularly the dictionary. For the next few hours I try to memorize new words and construct situations in which such words might be applicable. Just as I tone, trim and develop the muscles of my body, I need to do the same with my mind. Words are power; they capture things; sunsets, storms, people.

For half an hour of each day I am allowed to walk around the courtyard with an escort. This affords me the opportunity to breathe fresh, if not free, air. Once back in my cell I exercise for maybe another hour. Pull-ups and more stretching. I have reduced my needs to a minimum. I have no desire for alcohol, tobacco or junk. I have no affection for material objects. I have no emotional attachments to anything or anybody. Love is an emotion that I have learned to eradicate. There is nothing they can take from me, except of course my life. Well blood, dying is a part of living, admittedly the heavy part, but until you accept the inevitability of your death you cannot begin to live. Pop, I have learnt to discipline both my mind and my body. I want you to start to discipline your mind. Read Mao, Marx and Lenin. You will find them tough to begin with but persevere. You will be surprised. Suddenly, like a big cat breaking cover, the words rush towards you. It is important that our movement does not get stuck on 'black'; we need to move on to 'power' and these men know all about power. Try. Let me know how you get on. Maybe you and I can form a cadre of two. Now wouldn't that be something! Oh, and very important. Try not to sleep more than five hours a day. We are accustomed to too much sleep.

Later,

Rudy

February 1967

Dear Father,

What's going on? They must be seizing my mail. You know the regulations. I cannot imagine that you would write or send anything controversial. Are you ill? Southern winters can be deceptive. A chill is cutting through me right now. If you need the postage money for medication then don't write. I will understand. Make sure Moma wraps up well. If it gets rough then don't let her out to work. She can be stubborn. She continually blinds herself to the fact that historically they have tried to break our people like branches from a tree. Let the white woman tote her own stuff.

I got some good news. I've been down on Max Row four months. So you're thinking, 'what's good about that?' Well, only two more months of clean behaviour and I will be back in the general population. From there I can see the parole board in May, or June at the latest. Now, I've been thinking that what I ought to do is get a lawyer before it is too late. They got me transferred out here to Belsen on some trumped-up charge of assaulting a guard. Do you really believe that if I was provoked enough to attack a guard I would merely assault him? Lawyers cost money, but please try. I do not want to miss out on the next parole board. It is impossible to know to what depths these people might sink in their quest to break my spirit. Proper representation is required.

Over six years ago, as a nineteen-year-old manchild, I walked into a liquor store because I needed some bread. I could have wasted the pale who owned the joint, but I didn't. I could have taken out the two hick cops in their hicksmobile, but I didn't. Did I get any credit from the judge and jury? Not a damn thing. So I'm in prison for six years (so far!) for attempting to steal forty dollars. But they tell me that if I behave then I can get out. I think we have different concepts of the word 'behaviour'. The only way out of here for the black man is on his knees with his tongue scooping and looping along the floor. Some go out in boxes and directly to the morgue. Nobody walks out upright and tall like a man. It is against the rules. Deemed improper behaviour.

Moma should stop working for a few weeks. Make the people pay her some compensation for her toil and slavery. If they won't pay then you should go and take what is rightfully hers. The problem with America is that nobody dare confront the capitalist status quo. Other peoples of the world, the Chinese, Koreans, Cubans, Russians, they all cried as one, 'Enough is enough!' and punched the air with their clenched fists. In Africa, nation after nation is throwing up a revolutionary people who are seizing the steering-wheel and bumping the European off to the side of the road. What the white American needs is to taste the Mau-Mau spear. Pop, I want you to read a book called *The Wretched of the Earth* by a West Indian named Fanon. You will find it easier going than Lenin or Marx, but just as heavy. It is more up-to-date and written in less technical English. It concerns men of color directly. Nyerere, Kenyatta, Lumumba, all the great African leaders have used it as a manual. Some day you and Moma and Laverne and I will see Egypt and Ethiopia. But I think we should settle in Ghana, the mother-country of African independence. They have made it clear that there is plenty of land for us all, and the admission price is 'soul'! Damn, won't that be something to look forward to!

Yours,

Rudy

Dear Father,

Still no word from you or Moma. I wonder as I wander. I wonder if the pigs are trying to torment me? If so they will not succeed. I have learned to walk without emotional crutches. If I never hear from either of you again it will not hurt me. I will recognize it as part of the price I pay for being born a slave in America. But I will collect dues. The cell measures ten by four. The slave-catcher pigs are edgy. There is trouble upstairs in the main block. I can smell tear-gas. Men are not naturally brutal. It is their environment that makes them so. Life in prison is not like being inside the boxing ring, it is like being inside the boxing glove. I wonder if one of you is ill? If maybe somebody has had to be hospitalized and you are too busy seeing to their needs? If this is the case then I completely agree that you should channel all your energies into those who are more helpless than myself. Is it you who is ill, Pop? I wonder if Laverne wants to write her brother? Has she discovered the pleasures of bearing a man's weight? I suggest you talk to her on this subject. It is very important for a young girl to protect herself against both unwanted pregnancy and diseases of a sexual nature. Moma is a little conservative in this area, so the responsibility is yours. I wonder how Popa Williams is? Does he ever talk about me? I expect not. I regret not knowing your mother, my grandmother. You must be like her for you are not in any way like him. He represents an era of sloth and verb-busting decadence. He lacks your purpose. He used to anger me with his lazy eagle-eyed ways. I used to anger him with my youthful blackmanishness. But I wish him well. I wonder if in Nazi Germany they used to keep the lights on as a form of torture? When I first came on Max Row I thought I had hit a home run. The light upstairs in the main block was bad and went off at 10 p.m. I felt sure I was ruining my sight and would benefit from eyeglasses. But now I long again for some gloom. Have you ever tried to sleep under a bright lamp? I do not recommend it. I wonder if you have thought yet of a lawyer? I wonder if Aunt Sophie will come back? I wonder why as a child I always wanted the Indians to kick John Wayne's ass? I wonder why America is sending black men to kill yellow men to protect the capitalistic interests of white men? I wonder if you see my child? I wonder if Gwendolyn looks upon you as Femi's grandparents? Does she still call the girl Sondra? Femi must know that her father loves her. No matter what happens. Make sure she knows of me. Can you do this for me? I would do this myself but, as you know, I am legally denied access. They will one day learn that natural love is beyond legislation. I wonder if you might send me some nuts. They are good for protein. I am gradually trying to wean myself off prison food. A man can live on water and an adequate supply of protein. It helps to build discipline. I wonder if you will get this letter?

Yours,

Rudy

March 1967

Dear Pop,

It will come as no surprise that I have thought a great deal
about the letter that I am now writing to you. This is my fifth
attempt to get it right. After each previous failure I have medi-
tated for an hour in an attempt to clarify my mind. Right now I
think I am on the case so I'll let it flow.

Your letter cleared up the mystery of your silence. So Popa
Williams died and you had things to take care of. I can relate
to that. He was your father; he didn't have anybody else; it is a
humanistic thing you did. However, your analysis of his life is
way out of line and reveals to me serious flaws in your knowledge of American society and how the reality of this society
affects the lives of the African captives.

Popa was a slave, he behaved like a slave, he lived and died
like one, and the sooner our professional slaves die the better
for us all. Onwards towards the day of revolution. The uprising
will lead inevitably to liberation, both mental and physical. So
Popa Williams is dead. Let us give thanks!

What did Popa do with his life? I'll tell you. From the
moment he was able to rear up on to his hind legs he drunk
happily from the trough of slops that the white man offered
him. I am sure that sometimes he did not feel like sampling any
more swill, but he did not want to cause any trouble so he
lowered his snout back down and got on with business. The
slops gave him energy to work from sun-up to sun-down, and
provided him with a little surplus juice so he could hussle some
body off a chick come evening. Then, in the morning, he'd get
up, unhook his cap and jacket, hang up his dignity and his

73

mind, and slope out through the door to slave and giggle for the man.

One night Popa's seed touched bases with a smooth ivory egg and you was begat, Pop. Was this a moment for rejoicing? Did Popa Williams take a grip on his existence, mobilize mind and body, finally prepare to lock horns with the dilemma of being born an African in America. Did he acknowledge the fact that he would soon be responsible for steering a young soul through the minefield of American hypocrisy? Or did he buy a fifth of bourbon and get strung out? I'll bet the lame tried to build himself a mannish rep that night with stories of how he pumped himself a child. I'll give you confident odds that it was a Saturday night. Most of what history we have was miscreated on a Saturday night. You can just about rule out all the other days. He finished his bourbon and went to the dance hall. Skin me daddy-O! He was wired up and everybody was jumping. Then later that night he crawled back to his sty and tried to insert himself into your Moma's body just to make sure.

Whether slaving on a farm or living upstate in Birmingham in bombed-out, hollow-eyed buildings, the kind that people are always itching to torch for the insurance, Popa's attitude always remained the same: don't trouble the man and hope that he won't trouble you any more than he's doing already. Pop, he barely provided for you and Uncle George. You had to leave school at twelve and start providing for him, and to my knowledge he never did once express any feeling of regret over that. He probably took your educational demise as a sign that he could consider himself semi-retired. Well, did he ever express any regret?

As long as I've known the American world I've seen the black man offered only one role: that of the lazy, shiftless nigger. For hundreds of years the African has been America's greatest actor. But like so many, Popa never seemed to acknowledge that he could turn down the role. And now he's dead. Pop, I think this might be a fortuitous occurrence. Now you are truly the head of the family. Long live the king!

Your son,

Rudy

March 1967

Dear Moma,

So I upset Pop. Pop has a problem with me. Well I have a
problem with him and people like him. And I have a problem
with you too. You see life is full of problems, and only the
strongest survive. The strongest are not those who face their
problems, but those who erect structures to deal with their
problems, and then mount the structures. Only from the ramparts can a man see clearly. You and others like you would
have me and Pop – black men – in the gutter where we cannot
see anything but the hem of your skirt and the sole of the white
man's shoes. I will return to this.

So you baptized Laverne. Is this what Laverne wanted? She
is fifteen now, isn't she? Did you brainwash her into taking this
step, or perhaps you threatened to withdraw something that
she dearly treasures? This is an old and well-tried tactic. Does
this baptism make Laverne a Christian or does it simply make
you feel more respectable? Do you not listen to anything I say
to you? So many questions flood into my mind. I am squeezing
this pencil tightly. Anger is an emotion that I still grapple
with. It will take time for me to totally excoriate it from my
person.

Do you remember the letter I sent to you about a year ago in
which I brought up the question of religion? I told you then
that the only religion for the black man was an African religion,
preferably Islam. There is much to be said for possessing no
religious beliefs, but if this proves impossible then clearly the
one religion to be avoided is that of Christianity. But you
baptized Laverne a Christian! I wonder why in your God's

75

name I bother to write to you! I write with the dignity of a man who has time to reflect and read on elemental problems. I offer you support when you ask for it, and guidance when I think you are in need of it, but you choose to ignore me. I sit here in the darkness of constant light with you and Pop as my only corporeal links to a world I am over six years distanced from, and you trash my shared words as though they were the disposable utterings of a mad man.

You say you are worried about me. You say you went to see the pastor to talk about me. Moma, the pastor does not know me! When did he ever set foot in a high-security prison? Does he know that here in America there are concentration camps? And you went to talk with Mr Wilson my old schoolteacher! Moma, it was he who told me that I had some talent; that I might one day become a clerk. He did not mention doctor, lawyer, judge, professor, or nuclear physicist. A clerk. He wanted me to make peace with mediocrity (like himself). A quiver-livered fade is all your Mr Wilson is, and he has no right to pass judgement on me, and you've no more business talking about me to him than you have talking about me to the pastor.

The European raped, pillaged, and exploited our people with two instruments: the Bible and the gun. He walked into our lands holding up his book of religion but behind it he was toting a full and ready-cocked musket. Do you understand? And when you arrived on these Babylonian American shores he stripped you bare of your language – hence our communication in his tongue – and he took from you whatever form of African religion you might have had and replaced it with his own slavish worship of a white faggot woodsman with long hippy hair who messed with the Jews and got what was coming to him. Moma, ain't it ever struck you as strange that African people scrape their knees on the ground and wail and gnash their teeth over some dead white boy. Make more sense to me if we fell to our knees and worshipped images of Paul Laurence Dunbar. At least he's done something for our people. You ever read any of his poetry, Moma? No, I didn't figure so.

Moma, you're a woman. There ain't no women in this camp. Sure, they have women's camps, but the women in there are shackled for whoring, not warring. You're an African woman and you have to understand that the full burden of American society's dehumanizing bull falls on the African man's shoulders. He needs your support, not your scorn. You must take his advice, not listen to what he has to say and then act in a contradictory direction. That makes you a quisling and we must tear the hearts out of the bodies of such people. Your sister, Aunt Sophie, is a process-headed, ugly female quisling. Family blood can run deep. I am a literal and metaphorical prisoner, Moma. I need you to stand by me, not sit on me. I see little point in further communication between us.

   Goodbye,

Rudy

Dear Moma,

You must help Pop and not chastize him. He is weak. The death of Popa Williams has struck him hard. He who mounts the throne with confidence is a fool. Pop is not a fool. The mantle of this new responsibility sits heavily upon his shoulders. You must do what you can to ease the pain.

Life here is much the same. My studies are progressing. Have you thought of night classes, Moma? To acquire another language is to open a thousand doors on to the world. I suggest Chinese or Arabic. The etymological roots of both languages are buried in non-European soil. This is important. Are you looking after your body? Are your bowel movements regular? As one must purge the mind of garbage (comedy shows, comic books, ball games) one must also purge the body. Do not be embarrassed. In our native lands such questions are not considered impolite. They are as natural as asking somebody the time of day.

I require some additional material for my studies. *The Autobiography of Malcolm X*, Claude McKay's *A Long Way From Home*, anything by W. E. B. Du Bois, and as many black history books as you can lay your hands on. (You may experience some difficulty obtaining a copy of Claude McKay's *Autobiography* as it has been allowed to gather dust and fall into obscurity. But please try.) Second-hand editions of all these books will be fine. Please allow Laverne to peruse them for as long as she wishes. And, of course, Pop must study them before you send them on to me. When you do so mark clearly on the envelope what it is you are enclosing.

I am entering a very important phase of my development as I try now to marry my political reading with the African–American experience. I feel like a chemist holding two semifull test tubes, I have to decide which to pour into which. Either way there will be a reaction of some kind, perhaps a loud fizzing, perhaps an explosion, as a new substance is born. You will receive bulletins from my laboratory.

I am making ready to write Laverne whether you like it or not. I will send official papers to formalize the arrangement. Then she can be placed on my register. I expect you to acquiesce to my demands. Her situation will soon become desperate.

Your son,

Rudy

Dear Joe,

Can you not control Alice? Did you know that there is a type of insect – a praying mantis – so sick that the female of the species devours the male immediately after copulation? Think about that. You are in danger for your mind is full of fear of the female. I could see it in your eyes as you sat opposite me. It was good to see you but your demeanor was that of a man in a crisis. Pull yourself together, Joe. Hang in or hang up. Make up your mind. This situation is destroying you. Two more points.

First, your clothes. You dressed up in what you people call your Sunday best. Sunday has religious overtones and as you are aware I have no religion. That can wait until we return to Africa. Once there I will look around and see what is on offer. You could have come dressed as an ordinary slave-labouring man. There is nothing wrong with dirt. A little grime is the *sine qua non* of our bondage. The second point concerns your attitude towards the pigs. They are ready to wipe out a smoke on the smallest of pretexts. If they cannot find one, and they want to pop you bad, they make up a pretext, manufacture one out of thin air. They are the deadly enemy with whom I am engaged in mortal combat. Why then did you say more to them than was strictly necessary? Joe, you were polite! And these are the same men that would make obsolete your own son. If a pig thrusts a chair in your direction you sit on it – if you wish to take the weight off your weary limbs – or you ignore it. You do not say 'thank you' even if it is meant sarcastically. Such humour has no place in the day-to-day routine of the camps.

Please come back and visit, but come back as the strong natural African man you are, Joe, not as some knock-kneed, shoe-shuffling clown right out of a minstrel troupe. It makes them happy to see you trying to be somebody else in your Sunday best.

So Clytie is dead. Is there a plague on our family? A sister-in-law is an unchosen and easily disposable relative. Did you really know her? She lived a very simple country life. I think Laverne may have some residual affection for her. Personally I always related to George, although looking back I can see that he drank too much liquor and laboured under the misconception that the African's only hope for emancipation necessitated his relying upon benevolent white liberals. The truth is a millennium or two might pass before Mr Charlie would even notice that the African was waiting for somebody or something. George's philosophy is that of a 'Tom'.

Do you intend to take George into your house? I forgot to ask you this, but I would advise against your doing so. He is a country homeboy, a man unfamiliar with the concrete streets and urban hatred of Birmingham. The adjustment would be too great and it would distract you from your present purpose, which is to liberate your mind and lead your family by example. George has no family. (Was his bull-hood in working order?) Believe me, he will survive.

I can hear noise upstairs. The rhythms of the asylum beat with increasing ferocity. You commented on the noise. It is spring, I imagine the birds are singing. I trust that next year I will be able to see the April sunrise and sunset in an African locale. I trust that you and I will be able to walk across the plains as free men, looking and recognizing, reclaiming what is rightfully ours. Do you have any news about Rhodesia and the Union of South Africa? Again this is something I forgot to ask you. So much flies from my mind when faced with the reality of your presence. You have a powerful effect upon me, Joe. Turn your power on Alice. Make her see.

There is a slogan – perhaps you have heard it? – 'South Africa must be free by 1973!' Do you really think it will take the South African people that long to rid themselves of the white lice that infest their land? Do people imagine us so passive that we shall sit back and wait six more years (I will soon know all about six years!) before crushing the evil separatist regime. Rhodesia is a slightly different problem. In that country English hypocrisy is at work. Empire, or what they have left of it, has made them both greedy and intransigent. I need more information before I can hypothesize a solution.

Try to acquire the books we talked about. I am glad you find Mao's words of some value. Don't give up on Marx or Lenin. They are heavyweights. Once you have mastered them then all others will fall. Do not abandon the arena of combat. Let us talk also about Vietnam. I am pleased to hear it from you that you would have been against my being drafted. But would you have physically stopped me going, would you have given me money to dodge the draft, would you have hidden me in your rafters and fed me cookie chips and hot milk till this storm blew over? Or would you have blown away this President Johnson? Just how much against my being drafted are you, and what is your position on the war in general? These are questions we must debate.

Later,

Rudy

Joe,

I will not be able to explain everything. Should I try this letter will be seized and either returned to me or destroyed. Such is the nature of prison censorship. You must learn from now on to read between the lines of my work, to re-interpret my phraseology and pauses for in everything there is meaning. Something happened, I cannot say what. I was provoked and acted; I did not react. I will now be on Max Row for another twelve months. I was so close but they did not want me to make it back to you. They arranged it all.

Did I ever tell you what life is like here, Joe? Down here I have no television, no radio; I have no access to the gym, no day key so I can let myself in and out of the cell, no library, and no right to labour in the carpentry shops where I might make five cents an hour constructing garbage. I do, however, have paper and pencils which give me the strength to go on; take them away from me and I am nothing. Upstairs they can wear sweaters sent in from outside. A man's sweater is his badge of identity. It marks him out as somebody different. No two sweaters are the same. If somebody shows up with an identical sweater the two have to fight it out to see whose sweater will be destroyed. And I mean fight it out. The pigs make wagers on these bouts. They are fight promoters.

Pigs want the African prisoners to literally grovel at their feet. This makes them grunt and squeal with delight. The pigs play out their sexual fantasies in this way. I cannot elaborate. Understand what you will. White boys are often encouraged to take a detour past my cell. They carry slop buckets. They stop momentarily to pitch a curve-ball of excrement at me. The pigs laugh. This will happen once or twice a week. I am allowed to swab down my cell once a fortnight. Can you imagine? Pigs and white prisoners are all K K K types. If you are not of that psychological disposition when you come in, you sure are by the time they let you out. For white prisoners Belsen is a summer course in racialism.

Max Row is isolation. The deepest hell. No parole board will consider me from here. The pigs know this and have conspired to hold me captive for twelve more months because I refuse to bend. I am, in fact, unable to bend. Homo Erectus Africanus. Perhaps they do not know this. My cell contains an iron bed that is bolted to the wall. It is complemented by a cast-iron sink and a bowl designed to frustrate and choke and humiliate me. I do not know if I can survive twelve more months in the camp under these conditions. What about the lawyer? Is there not an attorney who would agree to one day being paid in African crops and fruit? Freezer techniques have come a great distance. It is possible to transport, in a frozen state, vast quantities of fresh produce. Make inquiries on my behalf. And please send me twenty-five dollars for cigarettes.

I have read W. E. B. Du Bois's *The Souls of Black Folk*. Did you read it, Joe? The pages looked uncut to me. In future I can wait until you have digested the book. That way we can build a dialogue around mutual reading. Why do you not mention Gwendolyn or my child? This fact causes me unnecessary worry. If you are attempting to spare my feelings then do not bother. My feelings are perfectly checked and in order. I am familiar with rejection.

Your son,

Rudi

Dear Joe,

Thank you for the photographs. The simple interplay of
light and dark on magic paper can be soothing, especially
when a man has nothing to look forward to outside of eleven
more months in this fearful zoo. I am trying to empty my mind
of expectations. I think this is where I have erred in the past
few months. Defective analysis made me weak. I was un-
prepared for the inevitability of the pigs' treachery. It was
stupid of me. The mistake of a manchild not the action of a
man. If you review and study my letters over the last six to
nine months I feel sure you will be able to trace my juvenile
descent into optimism. A revolutionary soldier should be ever
alert to the potentiality of ambush, particularly when stalking
in the jungle.

Alice looks happy. She has a smile upon her face. Did she
fashion it for the occasion or has it these days become a permanent part of her natural features? Her skin is richly textured,
but looks as though it could comfortably tolerate being dar-
kened a shade or two. A color photograph (which I understand
is not possible, nor am I requesting one) would clarify my
question: is Moma avoiding the sun? The sun's rays are harmful
if taken to excess, but in moderation they can add tone to the
skin and provide a source of energy for the body. It is one of
the first things that I intend to see to after I have walked like a
man out of this compound. I have a lot of sun put by in the
bank and I will be making some personal withdrawals.

You, Joe, you too look well. Just as I remember you from the
last visit, but this time I see you are wearing your hard labour-

ing clothes. Thank you. The appearance of your second chin is natural. I am glad to see that you have not adopted the common self-deception of wearing a beard. For a man of your years it only draws attention to yourself and makes people wonder just what it is you are trying to cover up. Who was the photographer and to whom did the camera belong? These are questions I need to know. They help to contextualize the photographs.

I am sorry that you have been unable to contact Gwendolyn, but I cannot believe that Alice has no means of reaching her grandchild. She is very fond of Femi, but perhaps she is holding out on you. I hope not. I met Gwendolyn when I was sixteen years of age. Do you remember? She was a comely, firm and salacious-looking fifteen. She and her Moma lived in a shot-gun shack (rent courtesy of the Jemisons) out towards Bessemer way. We were downtown folks compared to her and her Moma. Gwendolyn used to run with a partner of mine, a blood named Charles Louis McNorton. Crazy cat, would insist on being called his full name and beat up on anybody who refused to spell out all three parts loud and clear. Caught me good upside the head one time for calling him 'Charlie', but he backed down when he saw I was ready to duke with him and trade a few left and rights of my own. Anyhow, Gwendolyn was his squeeze until he got sent up for possessing a firearm with malicious intent. So, in accordance with the law of the tribe, I claimed the girl for myself. Night after night of irresponsible (sweet, but unprotected) jamming eventually paid dividend. She showed up one evening by the poolhall with her belly damn near busting out of her dress. 'Child,' I said, 'where in hell's name you been?' As you can imagine Pop, I could hear all the other fellars laughing at me, and I could see this fifteen-year-old girl had put me in a spot and everything, so I got mad as hell. I foolishly got into asking how she knew the child was mine, and accused her of playing around and so on. She started crying and I kept right on till she turned and Wilma Rudolphed it out of there. Well I took high-fives all around and the brothers gave me top marks for artistic impression. But inside I was worried for Gwendolyn. Later that night, when everybody had drunk their fill of beer, and the last frame was racked up and cannoned home, I took a walk over to her place. It was nearly morning by the time I arrived. I kicked on the door and her Moma opened up and pushed her dry-nappied head around the corner. She didn't need nobody to tell her who I was. She unhitched the door and let me in, then she went and woke Gwendolyn and made some hot strong coffee. We talked and I realized how decent the pair of them were. Two days later Alice hooked up with them and I think she was even proud of me for a minute. I had accidently stumbled across a decent girl. Pop, I will continue next week.

Your son,

Rudi

June 1967

Dear Joe,

Where was I? I think at the point when Alice met Gwendolyn and her Moma. I assume you remember when I took Alice around there. I was not trying to hide anything from either of you as I felt that I had only done what any normal man would have done. Popa Williams had some pietistical bull he tried to run by me about women taking away a man's strength and how I ought to keep clear of them. I figured he would rather have me married to a liquor bottle like himself, and make a goddamn pantomime out of my life. I looked back at him with as much contempt as I could muster, then I let him be before I got tempted to break a chair across his dumb head.

Alice and Gwendolyn's Moma came to some kind of understanding. They got so tight that the impending arrival of their first grandchild seemed to reduce them both to giggling schoolgirls. I tried to spend a little time with Gwendolyn at her home, but it was only then that I realized we had nothing in common. When she was on the streets, hanging out, disobeying her mother, she had something going for her, an attractive daring it was possible to dig. But now I discovered her hipness was stretched membrane-thin across an otherwise conservative personality. With her pregnancy the sheath had punctured. She was housebound and her dullness was exposed. It was then – I now recognize it as a desperate attempt to escape my total situation – that I tried to liberate some bread from a liquor store.

Well, I guess I'm not surprised that Gwendolyn does not want to see or hear from me again. But all I really want her to know is that Femi is still and always will be my daughter, even though I have never set eyes on the child. I want Femi to know that she is not Sondra, that her father is not a bum, he loves her, and that one day he will find a way of seeing her and making up to her for these many lost years. Joe, I do have to warn you that Alice may well be holding out on you. She is a woman and a mother, a doubly unpredictable combination. And she still sups deeply from the cup of ignorance. The African slave woman can be our greatest ally, but she can also be our greatest enemy for, unlike the white woman, she has access to 'soul' and can lure us into a false sense of security. A People's Court, along the lines of those that operate in China, would soon determine her guilt or innocence.

Has it ever occurred to you to wonder why no brother has ever put a hunk of lead into Bull Connor or George Wallace or the Grand Dragon of the K K K, or any of our more vicious and visible enemies? When I was up on the main block I used to hear brothers always talking about how they were going to get themselves a .45 smokeless and do the job themselves, but talk is not action and the job remains vacant. I have no answers on this subject and would benefit from your thoughts. One thing worthy of note as you sit down to wrap your mind around this conundrum, is to consider why a white man would want to shoot Kennedy? Is it because he 'helped' blacks? I don't believe he helped anybody but himself, but that is the image his public-relations men gave out. Public relations is a growth area. Hell, maybe that's what I need, not a lawyer.

And I want to hear more about this cat, Ali. I understand that last year he went over to London and knocked out some of those English boys. He is a phenomenon. First, he has given up on Christianity. This is a shrewd and correct private and public position for an African man to take. Second, he does exactly what he says he is going to do and makes no apologies for it. Third, he can articulate on issues beyond the ring with passion and intellect. They will hate him for his talent and I fear for his life. Do you really believe that the African slave will be allowed to act in such a manner? The pigs hate him. White folks hate him. Black folks must love him, but they must also love Sonny Liston. They must not fall into the white trap of thinking of him as 'a fat ugly bear'. Ali called him that for promotional reasons. Ali is his own public-relations man, and the best in the business! Secretly, in his heart, Ali recognizes Liston for what he is. A slave, labouring on the same plantation, in the same field as himself. Ali whipped his brother in order that he might speak from a position of authority. The champion has a captive audience; the challenger none. Any time Liston is in trouble, Ali will be there with a bucket and sponge and a pocketful of money. Send any press clippings, particularly interviews, that you can lay your hands on. Remember my words; it is only a matter of time before Ali returns to Africa for he is not happy in captivity. It is on African soil that he will truly flourish.

Twenty-three and a half hours is a long day. I have just smoked my sixtieth and final cigarette. It is approximately one in the morning. Upstairs it is three hours past 'lights out'. Down here it is neither daytime nor night-time. It is no time. To the barricades!

Your son,

Rudi

Dear Rita Mae Bailey,

So I have a 'Defense Committee' operating out of Birmingham! Thank you for coming to visit with me. If I appeared somewhat lost for words it is simply related to the fact that it is quite some time since I last laid eyes upon a pretty black woman. Do not misconstrue my words. They are not meant to be in any way offensive. I simply state a fact; you are beautiful. I spent more time looking than talking so I welcome this opportunity to briefly reintroduce myself and the details of my 'case' (as they insist on terming it). I am, of course, subject to all the usual restrictions of expression. Do you understand? Please make allowances for this in what follows

Name:	Homo Africanus
Occupation:	Survivor
Age:	200–300 years
Parents:	Africans captured and made slaves
Education:	American school of life
Distinctions/Awards:	Breath in my body
Recreation:	Not reading *Ebony*
Anything else of relevance:	I can dunk, punt and bunt. Sing, shimmy and slide. I can also kill, you dig?
The alleged crime:	At the age of nineteen manchild years I am supposed to have asked a white man, at the point of a .38, to pay some overdue wages. I did not harm a gray hair on his gray body. I

| | swear to God (a God) the man wasn't even scared. Probably thought that I was after candy. A posse of Feds blew in and for reasons I still don't follow decided to take me alive. They strapped my wrists and ankles to a pole and carried me off to their judicial feast. |
| *The punishment:* | One to life in a concentration camp of their own choice. 'The nigger was armed and extremely dangerous. Break him.' I am now doing six and a half to life. The self-fertilizing years and the life will soon fuse into one. |

Miss Bailey, I need a lawyer. You say you are trained in law. I do not understand why you should not be my attorney. You have never practised? Well practise now, practise on me. You say there are thirty people on my defense committee and you meet once a month. Please explain to the brothers and sisters that it is not possible for me to address each of them individually and so they must view this as a powerful love letter to them all. I appreciate the interest everybody is beginning to take in my case. Lord knows it is difficult enough being alone down here without also having to imagine that the world has forgotten you. But let us remember that for every Rudi Williams there are countless thousands in other cells, in other camps, in other parts of the United Snakes of America.

Why do our so-called 'prominent negroes' remain so muted, so luxuriously silent? Get Bill Russell to stop bouncing a basketball and start bouncing some heads. Get Jim Brown to rush them some news instead of rushing them a football. I am not expecting them to hijack the white media because that is all locked up in capitalistic paws. What these 'prominent negroes' should do is talk to our people. You see if our people get riled enough then we are bound to achieve almost anything we strive for. How's that, you figure. Well the white man is a materialistic capitalist. He built his country with the desire for property as the fundamental dynamic: remember, we were also property. Nothing scares him more than losing his property. So if I get mad and demand forty dollars of his property as back-payment he will react. If a thousand brothers get angry and begin to threaten a small town the white man is going to be fearful. If a whole nation of Africans gets vocal then the white man is going to come running with whatever he can lay his hands on to give us as a gift in order to prevent our wiping out his material stock. That is why the defense committee needs to operate laterally and demand either property or Rudi Williams. Just tell it like it is and stand back and take cover. The white man does not value me as highly as his more inanimate objects of wealth. At least not yet.

Yours sincerely,

Rudolph Leroy Williams

Dear Joe,

So George got himself a new woman already. Do you think he had her stashed away? Country foxes can do a beautiful job on a man's body: homeboy sure don't waste any time. Tell me something of your life with George as a child growing up. And don't leave out the humorous parts. I know there's got to be some. Have you read Richard Wright's *Black Boy*? Do so. You'll suffer the confusion of laughing and crying at the same time. These two emotions are closely connected. One leads smoothly into the other. Have you ever heard the term, 'I laughed until I cried'? And you must have observed brothers and sisters crying with grief who suddenly splutter into laughter. Joe, the Greeks had two faces for the theater. One with the mouth turned up, the other with the mouth turned down. The emotions are as closely related as that. I have spent too long with my mouth turned down. I still feel grief and frustration, but I have decided to approach life from the standpoint of joy. Let us practise this together. Let us both smile when you next find the money and the time to visit.

Could you send me either ten dollars or a carton of cigarettes? The carton must be open and the seal on each pack broken. This is to save the pigs trouble. I am not usually in the habit of aiding their foraging, but the dangers are obvious. They fear the smuggling of junk, particularly 'C' and horse. Cigarettes also have less camp value if tampered with. Thank you.

Just one more thing. In nine months I am due to transfer back to the main prison block. You know this, but in any case I remind you. Human memory is fallible. Joe, eventually I will see a parole board and Rita Mae Bailey has made it known to me that she can help on the legal side. What I will need, however, is for you to say that Alice and yourself are happy to take me in and support me. I will also need somebody to say that they are prepared to offer me a slave. Now it really doesn't matter what it is as long as it's legal, honest and will look good to the zoo-keepers.

Thank you for the clippings. I have no religion but I recognize him as a holy warrior in the tradition of the Muslims of North Africa who invaded, subdued, tamed, and educated the Spanish. If only he would turn his attention to Africa. He probably has enough charisma and power to disrupt the Union of South Africa single-handedly. His name literally means 'Praiseworthy One'.

Your son,

Rudi

Dear Laverne,

The papers finally got through! This means I can write to you and you to me. I assume this is what you want. You were nine years old when I was taken off the street. The judge ordered the overseer to transform me into a tame house nigger. So far they have failed, but the struggle continues. I was prepared for prison and consequently I have grown. Physically I am a healthy developed man. Mentally I am clear. Intellectually I am ever-expanding. You can turn any supposed disadvantage into an advantage given a plan. I will not waste precious time and space describing my conditions. I assume that over the years Joe or Alice will have shared at least some of my letters with you. If I am mistaken you must write me immediately and I will try to rectify the situation with a pen-portrait of the camp.

As a boy I used to sit you on my knee and I would tell you stories. Crazy bull I would make up, and you seemed to have a naturally receptive and finely tuned ear as far as such things were concerned. What I have done, in order that I might make our communication both informative and entertaining, is I have picked out a few of our African historical figures in the hope that we can rap about them. I have studied all of our African history in America to a depth at least equal to that of any professor in any university in the known world. My attitude to certain figures is made richer by my political leanings, which are, if we accept the simplistic left–right game that we are encouraged to trap our minds into, left – perhaps extremely left.

You might suggest, as we proceed, that I comment upon one or two individuals about whom you are curious. There is ample room for flexibility. I am not offering advice to you or lecturing you: this is a blood-brother and blood-sister pooling their minds. Remember, you will learn nothing at school once you have mastered reading and writing. Today the white man plays a cruel game upon us by bussing one or two African children to white schools and claiming these institutions to be 'integrated'. We accept this. Does he change the curriculum to allow for the presence of African children? Does he improve the facilities at the 'black' school? No. He does nothing that is not merely cosmetic. This suits his purpose and he successfully fools our more gullible people. As I said, you have learned and will learn nothing at school. Feel free to leave whenever the spirit takes you. Is your graduation certificate going to stop a pig popping you or Alice upside the head with his baton? Is it going to help free the African prisoners in America's jails? Is it going to bring Emmett Till back to life? Or heal the psychological wounds that are deeply burned into the soul of James Meredith? Is it going to enable Malcolm to speak again?

You should talk with Joe. He is developing by the week, but I sometimes wonder if he imagines he arrived here on the *Mayflower*. The lack of a strong black woman has often held back the African male. Where Alice has failed you might yet succeed. It often takes a woman to bring a man out of himself, but to do so the woman must be better than the man.

Coons, niggers, spades, darkies, spearchuckers. Do you recognize any of these figments of white folks' imaginations? They despise your durability, but to survive is not the highest morality. To survive with the will to begin again and go on, this is the highest morality. I have lived and died six or seven times in America, but how can they take from me my heritage unless I offer it to them like those fool 'Tom' diplomats who accept 'foreign' postings among their own people and talk over cocktails about last year's cocoa crop.

Sister soul, don't let no white man put you on display as a piece of freak tail. Be true to yourself. Power to the people.

Your brother,

Rudi

Dear Laverne,

Are you familiar with a man named Crispus Attucks? He lived from 1723 until 1770 and people say 'it' all began with him ('it' being the United States of America). However, his story is a short and sad one. He got himself killed outside the Customs House in Boston on a snowy March 5th in 1770. Let me give it a little context.

You see the British were running this place as a colony, hollering orders across the water, acting tall and making the settlers pay taxes for their tea. I mean these white settlers were not concerned with independence or anything, it was the idea of paying a little extra for a cup of tea that heated up their waters. On this March day a sentry was standing outside the Customs House trying to look cool – stiff upper lip and all that English reserve bull. Well there's not really much to do in wintry Boston so some pales decided to snowball the limey. He shouts to some of his kin for help and they come hightailing out from inside where they've been sitting down warming themselves and playing cards. Anyhow, what happened? Some say a soldier fell over and his gun accidently went off. Others say some limey just hauled up his musket and fired off a shot to scare people away. Now, whatever version you go with nobody disputes the fact that the limeys shot first. And who did they shoot? Yeah, a brother. All those tea-swilling, slave-owning, injun-killing, civilized white folk there and who did the British soldiers manage to shoot, Crispus Attucks, who I'll bet never drunk a cup of tea in his life. And that's how he became the first black hero of the United States, by standing in the way of a bullet.

So just what kind of a brother was this Crispus Attucks? People say he was born in some out of the way place named Framingham, Massachusetts, around about 1723, but you can never be too sure when we folks was born, same as you never know when it's a dog's anniversary. We was born to work, not eat birthday cake, and a lot of the masters and such they never stirred themselves to note down nothing like, 'Crispus, he's a Taurus and he likes wine, good clothes and fast cars.' The fact that there was another pair of legs running around the plantation was generally good enough news in itself.

Early on Crispus had a whole bunch of sense. You see he split: he ran away. Big fellar he was too, around about six two or three and weighed in the region of two hundred pounds when he made his move. This was in 1750 when by my reckoning he would have been about twenty-seven. Anyhow, the brother heads north and ends up hanging around Boston docks, acting the fool, jive-talking with people, shooting the breeze, and learning what it's like to lie in after six in the morning and not have to pick no more cotton.

One day Crispus is strutting down King Street (they call it State Street now – I suppose there's no need to explain why) when he bangs up against these limeys. Now, what he finds strange is that they all have their guns out and are standing up in front of the Customs House looking bad. Some versions got it like Crispus was leading a whole group of people down there shouting, 'Do not be afraid. They dare not fire.' Well, I'm kind of hoping that Crispus didn't say that thing. I mean they were soldiers, it's their job to kill people, and sure they dare fire, especially when all that's coming at them is abuse, the odd stone, and a volley of snowballs. No contest. But these heroic versions go on, and they got Crispus standing at the head of the queue and everybody behind shouting, 'Fire! Fire! and be damned.' Now I don't know how Crispus felt but it don't sound fair to me. You got these musket-wielding limey soldiers staring at you, and a whole posse of people behind you (check – behind you), and they're all shouting, 'sure, go ahead and shoot'? Next thing that happens is a stick sails through the air and strikes a Private Hugh Montgomery upside the head. At this point the top man, Captain Preston, tells Hugh to go to work. And who does Hugh shoot? Well I'll tell you who Hugh doesn't shoot, and that's the white boy at the back who boomeranged the stick.

Laverne, hold on. To be continued.

Your brother,

Rudi

August 1967

Dear Laverne,

I cannot believe a word of this Crispus Attucks 'hero' business. A brother takes all that time and uses up all his energy to run away, through the marshes with dogs and stuff on his tail, crossing rivers to try and throw them off the scent, spending the night up in trees, snitching food from barns; man, he didn't come north on no Greyhound bus. He gets to Boston and starts to hang out, dig chicks, doing nothing by fractions, taking a few drinks, then one day he is two-legging it on King Street walking off some whiskey, and he finds himself at the head of a group of people toe-to-toe with some soldiers, and everybody's shouting 'Fire!' and the brother doesn't even duck?

There is so much to say. I was hoping that I might try and confine my comments on each person to one letter to prevent these stories becoming too episodic. A week is a long time to wait for a conclusion. In future I shall be more concise. I was pleased to receive your letter. Your handwriting is bold and clear which suggests a confident and well-rounded personality. You were right to refrain from comment upon Crispus Attucks until I had finished what I had to say. Now that I have I look forward to your next dispatch.

It is hardly surprising that Alice has taken fright at our communicating so freely with each other. Has she explained to you what it is that she fears? I do not believe she has asked herself this question so you may well be doing her a great service by making her confront this grievance in her soul. I am sorry to learn of her ill-health, but a life of toil and slavery makes many demands on the human body. She should consider

101

indulging in a period of total rest. I will write to Joe and encourage him to temporarily redouble his work effort to afford Alice time to recuperate.

You mention that Mr Wilson has in the past spoken with you about something called 'Black History'. He knows nothing of history, and in spite of his skin color he knows nothing about black. His history celebrates black people's contribution to the building of a house they are not allowed to dwell in. It is true that we invented all kinds of things from the potato chip to the pencil sharpener, the overshoe to the corn harvester, but what of it? There is nothing culturally significant about an overshoe. Some day somebody would have invented it for it is a practical, functional, and logical addition to American life. Why pump up one's chest because it happened to be a black man? Unless, of course, you are surprised that black men should possess the ability to do such things. If a dog were to suddenly take the wheel of a Cadillac would Mr Wilson want to organize a 'Dog History' course?

Mr Wilson claims to be a teacher. The state is happy to pay him to function as such for them. We are happy to watch him malfunction as such for us. Has he completed his book? Has he ever mentioned to you or Alice or Joe his book? Perhaps he has given up on the book (or the book on him). He told me – when I was your age – that it was to be a history of negro theatrical entertainment from cakewalking through ragtime to minstrelling. I have done some research in this area. These American shows contained a farrago of songs with perfidious titles such as 'Rufus Rastus', 'Coal Black Rose', 'If the Man in the Moon were a Coon', 'All Coons Look Alike to Me', 'The Funny Little Darkies', 'We Never Fade', and so on. Mr Williams invests his energies in 'celebrating' 'Black History'. And Mr Williams is a teacher. I have never once heard the word 'Africa' fall from the lips of this Mr Williams. Be ever vigilant.

Your brother,

Rudi

Dear Joe,

Rita Mae Bailey has again been to visit with me. Where does she get the money from for these visits? Have you seen her? Is there really a 'Rudi Williams Defense Committee'? Who is this woman? You see, old friend, I have to admit that I simply sit and stare at this beautiful African vision and try to control the stirrings at the base of my belly. It goes without my saying that to do so is impossible. This is an involuntary muscle and as such a dangerous and uncontrollable part of one's anatomy. She is truly an ebony goddess worthy of deification. If you do not know her I suggest you try to make her acquaintance and talk with her of me. I will leave the details of what to say up to you, but one thing I will need upon my release next year is the companionship of a sturdy-minded sister.

Last night I dreamed of her. Masturbation has played little part in my life during the last seven years. This is not because I have any objections to it as a manly pursuit. On the contrary, I think the African man does not masturbate enough. It is a healthy form of release for emotional and physical energy. It can also help reduce the temptation to execute acts of infidelity with other sisters. Too much promiscuity dissipates energy, confuses the mind, introduces guilt, nullifies action. Masturbation is safe, quick and can be practised with little danger to self or others. Of course, the only drawback is that it places too much emphasis upon the actual moment of orgasmic ejaculation, an emphasis which if transferred to the body of the woman can lead to selfishness and an unsatisfactory performance on the part of the male.

One of my earliest experiences of a sexual nature was with Aunt Bea in Atlanta. Before I go any further I think it best you keep the information I am about to reveal to yourself, as Moma may be shocked to hear that her own sister played womanly host to my manhood. I was sixteen at the time and already had much experience under my belt, both in Birmingham and in the country at George and Clytie's. I felt bullish, confident, and sure of my powers – more so than I do now. I wanted to see Atlanta and obviously Alice thought it best for me to stay by Aunt Bea. She met me at the Greyhound station, a buxom woman, breasts like melons, firm and high and rounded. We took a bus back to her apartment, a small concrete block a mile or so from downtown. She gave me a key and asked me how long I intended to stay. I told her two to three days, but all I wanted to do was explore the city and look around. She drew a map of places that she thought might interest me, churches, bookstores, poolhalls (yeah, she was hip right off), and said I should come and go as I pleased. Naturally, I didn't ask her if she had a man or nothing, but on that first night I sure heard somebody in there firing on all cylinders with her. In the morning I heard the man's voice as he left. I figured Aunt Bea had a little something that probably belonged to somebody else. She had to be cautious.

Nothing much happened until the last evening. I was scheduled to take a bus at seven in the morning. I got in a little juiced up around eleven. Aunt Bea had taken a bath. I could smell her. When I saw her those big breasts of hers were busting out of her cotton nightdress. I felt myself jump and watched her eyes watching my root. Well, the rest is history. I made the bus and slept the whole journey back to Birmingham. She had me holding on all night, bulling and bucking this way and that. By the time we reached dawn I could barely step down off the bed I was so beat, but I knew I was a man. I had ridden and been rode and I felt a deep pride in my achievement.

Rita Mae Bailey has some of Aunt Bea's qualities. Not physically – in this respect Miss Bailey is far superior to the eye. But they are both determined African women who know what they want and will fly hawk-like towards the object of their desire.

Such women are rare in an American context. Joe, I need to know more about Miss Bailey. There are some things that men must do for each other.

How is Moma's illness? You did not mention this at all. I have an injury to my arm which accounts for the deterioration in my handwriting. I cannot explain how I came by the injury but it will take some months to heal.

Your son,

Rudi

Dear Joe,

Please explain to Laverne that I will write to her next week. I am sorry that she will have to wait another seven days but I have waited almost seven years and may have to wait seven more. Patience is a virtue that needs to be cultivated. When it finally pullulates it casts a peaceful aspect over your soul. Laverne is a beautiful woman. Thank her for the photograph.

Joe, I have to explain myself. As I do so you will perhaps come to realize what it is that I have been going through. The pigs have gone mad. They openly taunt me. Names have never bothered me – as weapons they are neither sharp nor blunt. I have a mastery of their language far in excess of anything they might achieve. But these days they enter my ten by four cell at will and scatter my papers, destroy my books, and then withdraw laughing and claiming that they did not find what it was they were looking for. Clearly it is a recognizable me that they are looking for. But because I refuse to genuflect before them, because I refuse to wear the garb of humility and stretch out rug-like so they might wipe their feet on me, it appears that I am doomed to suffer their constant visitations. My routine of work, study, sleep and exercise is now impossible. I sleep when I can, study and work when I can, and exercise with what little energy I have left.

Is this America, the civilized country of satellites and color television? Of Hot-Dogs, Coca-Cola, and Mickey Mouse? What dark part of this bright nation have we been condemned to, Joe, you and I? We must flee and burn bridges behind us as we leave. We are Africans. If we want our children to visit a Disneyland then let it be our own African Disneyland. The dice are loaded, the terms are unacceptable, the American odds too long.

I am somewhat ashamed of my last letter. Its tone was born out of my current predicament. But not that alone. Is it good for me to see women? I am not sure that it is. I have forgotten how to behave both with and towards them. They are delicate receptacles for love and pleasure, and vessels into which we might place ideas and see them flourish. However, if we are too hurried or too boorish they will break. Is Rita Mae Bailey a strong enough woman for me, Joe? Does she understand how unpractised I am in the sublime arts of courtship?

There is something that might shock you, Joe. Most of the captives, black and white, are faggots. Homosexuality is a sick but everyday fact of life in the camps. A newcomer who is unaware of this fact places his life in mortal danger. He is bound to be propositioned within hours of his arrival, and how he deals with this first approach is crucial to his future anal safety. It may be in the exercise yard, in the mess-hall, in the workshop, the television room or the toilet, but a man, sometimes more than one, will approach and touch you on the arm. He knows you are fresh blood and he is making his play. He will ask you if you need a friend. This is an ambiguous question. You may appear puzzled. He will ask again, only this time he holds your arm. This is the time to act. You must clench up your fist and crash it into his face. It does not matter how much stronger the man is, or how bad a beating you subsequently take, the fact is you must make public your violent rejection of such a vile offer. You must overreact to a homosexual proposition. To appear confused or frightened means that your manhood will probably be taken against your will. Maybe not then, but sometime in the near future. And they say that once you have been penetrated it is always easier to accept it a second time, and then a third, and a fourth will follow until you are a snivelling faggot pervert ready to go down on anything or anybody in exchange for a pack of cheap cigarettes or a wet from a bottle that contains an alcoholic beverage.

Do you still get pleasure from Alice or do you masturbate?

As your son it is important for me to know this as you, Joe, have travelled a path I have still to tread. Do not let the bushes close behind you and obscure my route.

I need a pair of shoes if I am to endure the winter months. Black, leather uppers, the quality of the sole is of secondary importance. Size nine and a half. I may also need eyeglasses. I shall ask the pigs to arrange a test. The light is burning my eyes and I fear I shall soon be left with two ash-lined and empty sockets. My arm is still painful.

Your son,

Rudi

Dear Laverne,

You pose a very interesting question about Crispus Attucks. I can find no reference to his parents, but it would appear that he had a brother named Prince. Beyond his 'name' I can find no further information as to his age, status, occupation (if not simply that of a chattel slave), or his opinions about his brother Crispus's life and death. Some of my books are missing, others out of date. It may be possible for you to find the information for yourself.

Phillis Wheatley (1753–84) forms a bridge. She was born in the old place, back in Africa. However, she seemed to take a shameful pleasure in saying to people that all she remembered of the continent of her origin was that her mother used to pour out water 'before the sun at its rising'. The picture becomes clearer when you read her poetry.

> *T'was mercy brought me from my Pagan land,*
> *Taught my benighted soul to understand*
> *That there's a God, that there's a Saviour too:*
> *Once I redemption neither sought or knew.*

Well, quite frankly, I think we have a problem here.

At seven years of age the African child arrived in America and was purchased from a Boston slave block by a rich merchant, name of John Wheatley. As some kind of social experiment Wheatley and his wife (Susanah) taught the child to read and write. Within sixteen months the 'American girl' ('Phillis') was reading Milton, Pope's translation of Homer, and the

Bible. By the time she was fourteen she had written a blank verse eulogy of Harvard University. By the time she was twenty she had written enough so that she was not only nationally famous, but known abroad as well. In 1773 she got her first book published, *Poems on Various Subjects, Religious and Moral*. They say it was the first book by an American black woman, and the second book by an American woman, period. Perhaps now that she had achieved manumission she considered herself to be American. She certainly penned a eulogy to 'His Excellency General Washington', George by name, slave-owner by hobby, President by occupation, and was entertained by him and by the aristocracy in England on one of her visits there. But what was with this girl? Did she never feel like pitching this whole bunch of neo-classical bull out of the window? Were there no mirrors in the house?

When John and Susanah Wheatley died Phillis found herself alone and poor. They did not provide for her. According to all accounts she was a good-looking sister, though slightly built and a little delicate of constitution. She soon met and married a brother 'name' of John Peters, a big handsome grocer whose main-line was popping style. He wore a wig, carried a cane, and liked to play the gentleman among his own people. He cared little or nothing for the white man, and this naturally brought him into conflict with Phillis. They had two children, who both died, and then a third. Life was not easy for either of them, and then one day Peters just upped and left. Now before you come down heavy on the brother with your 'typical!' bag, bear in mind that Phillis might have been disrespecting him as much as he was obviously disrespecting her. So what if he did not know his Pope from his Vatican – who gives a damn. He left Phillis in a boarding-house, where she eventually had to take a job scrubbing floors. In December 1784, at the age of thirty-one, both she and her child died of cold within a few hours of each other. Sad, but true.

Look around you, Laverne. You can see Phillis Wheatleys every place, old and young, men and women, African people who get taken up by the white man and swallow anything that he tells them. Then when he puts them down – which he surely will – they have too far to fall and nobody to catch them. Is this not what happened to the pugilist Floyd Patterson? And I fear such big-mouths as Sammy Davis Junior and other 'entertainers' I could mention will fall heavily. Find yourself in the bosom of your own people. You may be misunderstood, but you will be misunderstood by people who in their own frustrating, selfish, and often ignorant way, do care.

Your brother,

Rudi

Dear Joe,

I write to wish you a happy fifty-first birthday. Considering the ongoing struggle of this life, I am not sure how much significance the African man should attribute to such days. We are literally asked to rejoice and acknowledge the day of our birth. This is connected with the whole notion of being released from the captivity of the womb. Now it is true that we African people were, like the white man, released from the captivity of the womb but, unlike the white man, we were released only into the greater captivity of American society. It goes without saying that our true birthday will be celebrated on the day we step out of our American exile into a different and fuller form of freedom. In future years we should think of dating our individual birthdays from the moment we again set foot on African soil.

I received both of your letters on the same day. Either the postal system is defective, or you wrote the letters concurrently. It is difficult to decide which, for you do not date either letter. In future you might consider dating all your letters as a precaution against further confusion.

It is very pleasing to learn that you are now enrolled in a night-school class taking automobile maintenance and servicing. To be honest I would have preferred you to be involved in something a little more political, but the discipline of regular study will be of value. You may eventually graduate your class and move into languages, philosophy, or even agricultural science. In the short term, automobile maintenance and servicing can be of infinite value. Should you be made redundant

112

from your present slave, then you can always pick up work in the neighbourhood. You might also find it possible to purchase a cheap car and take Alice for country rides. You might even consider driving down here to visit me a little more often. This is not a complaint. I know you come as often as is possible, but it is a fact that it would be pleasant to have the opportunity of seeing you more frequently. Automobile engineering is a trade you might one day teach me – we might consider raising the capital for our passage and land by opening a small garage business. Your night-school ambitions may yet open doors for us both.

Within twelve months of my being involved with you in a garage business you would be able to retire for I possess the necessary positive attitude and vulpine business skills to outstrip any rivals. To help accelerate the processes that could lead to my release from this camp, you may find among your fellow students one who might be prepared to consider me as a future employee. If they intend to be, or are already involved in the garage trade, then so much the better, for it will allow me the opportunity to study their modes of operation and apply the knowledge to the practical realities of our own business.

I will be twenty-seven years of age when I leave behind my chains, for it is only my chains that I shall leave when I walk out through the gates. My soul, manhood, and pride go with me. Only five more months down here before I am returned to the main block. My recent good conduct record will mean a parole hearing and a release date. My arm is a little easier. I can bend it now.

Your son,

Rudi

Dear Joe,

I have recently received a troubling letter from the 'Rudi Williams Defense Committee'. No, the letter is not from Miss Rita Mae Bailey, although it is clear from the handwriting that it is she who penned it. However, the letter is officially sent by, and intended to be received from, the whole committee.

What troubles me about the letter is that it is all talk with no mention of impending action, and even worse, no mention of any real desire to, or knowledge of how to, act. I am a man in solitary confinement. Here I meditate when the pigs allow it, but I have no way to act. I have to rely upon the goodwill of others. This is the nightmare of my life. Out there I acted and had no time for meditation. Here I meditate but I have no way to act. It is in the interplay of the two that one creates the whole man. I now recognize this and feel stronger and better prepared for what remains of life's struggles. But why does this committee simply talk, hold meetings, talk some more, write me the odd letter, and talk some more? What about action? What about marching and protesting and burning and shooting a few people? What about getting all sore in the throat and purple in the face? What about taking the bat to the ball and opening your shoulders? I might die mentally or physically and Miss Rita Mae Bailey would still be sending me letters about the minutes of the last meeting as though I were a stock-market commodity. For God's sake, Joe, can you not make these people understand that I am a man who demands action!

Did you speak with Rita Mae Bailey like I asked you to? And if so what did you say? The new tone of her communication is cold so I fear you must have said something that disturbed her. I trust you had the presence of mind to say nothing about the dream that I shared with you. Whatever it is you said (if indeed you spoke with the sister) has changed her attitude. Perhaps it is my mistake for asking you to speak with her. There are some things that a man must do alone.

And so this ugly question of integration has reared its head in the context of your night-school classes. Do they seriously imagine that by having ten black and ten white students they are advancing the cause of racial harmony in America? Surely it breeds a deeper resentment when these artificial attempts at race-mixing are force-fed to both the white man and the African. Malcolm has some particularly pertinent words on this subject.

> The truth is that 'integration' is an image, it's a foxy Northern liberal's smoke-screen that confuses the true wants of the American black man. Here in these fifty racist and neo-racist states of North America, this word 'integration' has millions of white people confused, and angry, believing wrongly that the black masses want to live mixed up with the white man.

What Malcolm is saying is that the white man fears integration because he assumes it means we will eventually (because he assumes we want to) bed his women. This is, of course, not true, but the white man lives in his own unshakeable fantasy world. When you speak to most African-American men the failure of integration as a viable social experiment becomes startlingly clear. Most of us don't want a damn thing to do with them over and above the minimum contact necessary to limp from one slave day to the next. Nearly any African man will tell you this. We do not want to be integrated into their lives any more than they want to integrate with us. In my short life on this wretched American soil I have never known natural integration. The hospital in which I was born, the neighbourhood I grew up in, the schools I mis-attended, the shops, bars, poolhalls I hung in, the cats and chicks I dug, the camps I've been in (including the one I send this letter from), they were,

115

and are, all segregated as much by choice as by law. That is just how it was, how it is, and how it always will be in America. From your letter I gather that neither the brothers nor the pales are happy about this ten-ten thing. Then why do it? Who are the state government trying to impress? This is the sad madness of race-hypocrisy in America.

How is Alice? I will write if she is well enough to reply. Otherwise I will wait until you think it appropriate for me to put pen to paper. You may not have a letter from me for a few weeks as I am anxious to complete Laverne's 1967 semester. I am proud of the way you have developed in the last few months. I am interested in the social significance of the ownership of different types of motor-car. Do you think you might look into this area for me?

Your son,

Rudi

December 1967

Dear Laverne,

Picture a Caribbean island with mountain ranges that lever up to over 6,000 feet in places, whose slopes and valleys and plains hold and reflect a burning tropical heat. Half a million brothers and sisters live in this place where slavery is a serious business. We are in the eighteenth century and this island of San Domingo is the richest colony in the world. The French are digging it, but a brother is about to stride on to the scene and organize what the white man thought was impossible: a successful slave rebellion. Africans in America had tried. The first major rebellion was in New York City in 1712. I can just picture it, a whole posse of bloods charging down Fifth Avenue demanding a piece of Macy's. And later on there appeared head trouble-makers like Gabriel Prosser, Denmark Vessey, and good old Nat Turner. Some white man just came up with a book on Nat, tried to make out he was an invert. I mean how can a goddamn brother who kicked (not pumped) ass be an invert? Still, the fact remained that none of these brothers were as bad as our San Domingo man, a brother named Toussaint L'Ouverture (1746–1803). One thing he had going in his favour was the size of the island. You could look up from the cane-field and out over the sea and dream of pitching the master or overseer or both into the water. And the island was small enough to conceive of taking it out in one go. But upstairs in America, you dust somebody off in North Carolina then his cousin from South Carolina, his brother from New York, and his sister's husband from Georgia will all soon be on the scene to discipline you.

117

W. E. B. Du Bois said that 'The role which the great Negro Toussaint, called L'Ouverture, played in the history of the United States has seldom been appreciated.' He so worried the English that they started up their anti-slavery movement. He worried the French leader Napoleon so bad that he sold Louisiana and gave up his dream of an American empire. And he worried the southern white man to the extent that he immediately cut down on the number of Africans he was importing because he did not want to get outnumbered like in San Domingo. And what did this powerful African achieve? Well, he was the architect of the first black American state, called Haiti. Its creation involved the beating up of the local whites, then dusting the French, the Spanish, and the English by the employment of superior military thinking and fighting with greater determination. Never let anybody tell you that the odds are too long. Anything can be achieved given the right mental attitude.

Toussaint's father was the son of an African chieftain – in other words he was real people over there. But he got himself captured, sold off as a slave, and shipped to San Domingo. A French man bought him and must have seen something noble in his demeanor because he set up Toussaint's old man with a plot of land and five slaves for himself. Then the old man takes up Catholicism, gets married, and has eight children the oldest of whom is Toussaint.

Toussaint grew up to be an educated and reserved family man who commanded the respect of all who knew him. It was when he was forty-five, gray-haired and set in his ways, that trouble started in San Domingo as the brothers began to lose patience with the system of slavery they were chained to. They formed an army of sorts and Toussaint joined up and was soon running the situation. He liked especially to include the African-born brothers, figuring rightly that they had more sense of what they had lost and therefore more idea of what they might gain. Before you knew it victory began to back up against victory and Toussaint made himself General. He was now controlling San Domingo as all the white folks (both local and foreign) had been defeated. This is where he made his first and

118

only mistake; an egregious blunder for one so otherwise astute.

In order to consolidate his victory Toussaint decided to travel to France and make a deal with the notorious nigger-hater, Napoleon Bonaparte. Toussaint's number two, Dessalines, said 'no', but Toussaint went and they locked him up, humiliated him, then allowed him to starve and freeze to death. Meanwhile, Dessalines declared Haiti an independent black state, himself Emperor, and massacred the whites which ensured there could be no more slavery. Toussaint was decisive in everything until the moment when he had to consolidate his power: it was then that he foolishly looked for white approval. He was a fighter with home advantage until he went to Europe. It does not pay to rely upon these out-of-town judges.

Why is it that even the finest, most powerful and intelligent of our African people still find it necessary to look for the white pat on the back? This is a mystery to me and causes me much grief. Surely it is not too abstruse a question for our prominent minds to grapple with? We need answers. If you feel you want to do something, Laverne, then let your positive attitude take you the whole way, not just a part of the way. This is one of the lessons that we might draw from the story of the courageous West Indian African named Toussaint L'Ouverture. Do not stop in mid-flow to reason with the enemy. Do not let anybody take your dream. Be ruthless in the achievement of your goals.

Your brother,

Rudi

Dear Laverne,

You say that I am unnecessarily critical in my summary of
the character and life of Phillis Wheatley. That perhaps I do
not fully appreciate the circumstances of the black woman's life
and how she has had to adapt and deal with, as you put it, a
more degrading type of history with reference to slavery and
racism. You are a young woman of sixteen and it is good that
you are thinking about such things. But do you really believe,
as you say, that the African woman has had to endure more
than the African man? You are not querulous by nature so I
imagine you must believe your hypothesis. However, I shall
challenge you.

Surely the removal of the tradition of male responsibility for
the family hurts the male pride more than that of the female. A
psychological adjustment of massive proportions is demanded
of the African male. I cannot believe that the female has to
make an adjustment of greater magnitude than the male, although I do accept that the female soul must also be bruised in
a way not too dissimilar to that of the male. How does this
affect their achievements? Well it depends upon each individual's character. There are examples of male Phillis Wheatleys. Perhaps you can think of some? If you truly believe that
the African woman has suffered more, and presumably by
extension deserves a different critical approach, then you must
explain in greater detail the nature of your objections. I risk
further chastisement by looking briefly at the life of another
African woman, Harriet Tubman. I will give only the bare
outline of her life and try to refrain from too much sermonizing

in the hope that you will make yourself clear in your next letter. By doing this I also hope to avoid causing any further offence. It is, however, worth reminding you that I am not a hagiographer.

The 'Black Moses' of her people was born Araminta Ross in Dorchester County, Maryland. Nobody really knows why she changed her name to Harriet Tubman, but we do know she was badly beaten by her masters and sustained serious scars and bruising to her neck, back, and head. In 1849, aged twenty-five, she upped and split along with two of her brothers. They hid out in caves and graveyards, dodged dogs and wild men, waded water, and lay low in marshes until they reached so-called 'Freedom City', Philadelphia. I say so-called because at about the time Harriet was entering the city brothers were tearing up the place, grabbing guns, bricks, paving stones, and sticks, and fighting back against the whites in a bitter riot that lasted over twenty-four hours. For a minute Harriet must have wondered if she'd arrived in the right place. But when all the uproar blew over she realized that she was better off up north than down south, and she figured it her duty to help lead others out. She had parents, a couple of kids, and some sisters and brothers still doing time down there. So instead of just cooling it, she started to return back south and lead people north to freedom on what they came to call 'the underground railroad'. Others were engaged in the business, and Harriet was by no means responsible for its inchoation, but she became its most famous practitioner, possibly because she was such a small woman with such a big heart. They called her 'Moma Moses', leading her people north to the promised land.

Her method was simple. She would send messages down by word of mouth: 'Tell my brothers to be always watching unto prayer, and when the good old ship of Zion comes along, to be ready to step aboard.' Folks would get together in little cabins, iron pots turned upside-down for seats, and they would plan who was going to go up north. By and by a song would rise in the bush: 'Get on board, little children. There's room for many a more.'

Nineteen times she made her pilgrimage down south in the

121

years before the so-called emancipation, and in all she brought back over three hundred brothers and sisters to New York, Philly or Boston. After 1850 there was a law passed called the Fugitive Slave Law which meant Harriet preferred to lead her people the whole way up to Canada instead of fooling around and trusting Uncle Sam. Despite the forty thousand dollars on her head she was never betrayed or captured. If a baby cried and looked like it might give them away then she would pour opium in its throat. If an old man got tired or sick and said he could not make it she would cock her pistol at his head and say, 'Dead niggers tell no tales. You go on or die.' That's what I call a positive spirit. I hope my story has not been unnecessarily critical for your tastes. I have tried to present the facts as they are known to me.

Your brother,

Rudi

Dear Laverne,

I have made a pledge that one day we must visit our cousins in the West Indies. Their history is our history for they too are African people captured and sold into American bondage. They were shipwrecked on American islands, we on the American mainland. While the white men who 'owned' us became American, their white men remained Europeans: French, English, Spanish or Dutch. The African West Indian is a captive within a captive and colonial society. We are captives in a supposedly free society. But we are historically of the same blood. What is inimical to them is inimical to us also.

I have spoken already of the great West Indian, Toussaint, but there is a Jamaican named Marcus Moziah Garvey (1887–1940) who came very close to achieving what would have been the greatest coup of the century. Instead he died broken, alone and forgotten in London, England. Such is the nebulous line between success and failure.

In 1916, aged twenty-eight, Garvey strode into Harlem. In his native island he had founded the Jamaica Improvement Association, based on the teachings of 'Uncle' Booker T. Washington, but it had failed and he left for New York. He joined the soap-box orators on the broad streets of Harlem, and people listened for he had a powerful voice and a great presence. However, and most importantly, people listened because he was saying what they wanted to hear. He made certain declarations. First, that black stands for strength and beauty. Second, that blacks should be proud of their noble past and ancestry. Third, that the white man has racial prejudice so deeply

123

wrapped up in his system that it is a waste of time appealing to his sense of justice or democracy – self-determination is what is needed. Finally, that the only real hope for black men is to go back to Africa and build up a country there that everybody might return to.

Marcus started up an organization called the Universal Negro Improvement Association which by the middle of 1919 had thirty branches and, so Garvey claimed, a membership of four million. He probably exaggerated a little, but he did create powerful offshoots such as the Universal Black Cross Nurses, the Universal African Motor Corps, the Black Eagle Flying Corps, and, most famous of all, the Black Star Steamship Line. Garvey invited subscriptions in the Black Star Steamship Company to be purchased in shares through the mail. Between 1919 and 1921 he collected over ten million dollars and spent over one million buying and equipping ships. But by now America was running scared of him. In 1923 they put him on trial and a federal judge sentenced him to five years in an Atlanta pen on a trumped-up charge of using the mail to defraud. In 1927 he was pardoned but they still shipped him back to Jamaica as an 'undesirable alien'. He tried to rebuild his 'Negro Zionism' from a Jamaican base but he confronted an excess of apathy. His life never recovered. He came within an ace of organizing a mass exodus to Africa, but had victory snatched away when almost in his grasp.

Garvey was not always the most subtle of men. For instance, his African Orthodox Church had the angels and the Virgin Mary depicted as black, and Satan and the imps as white. He declared himself 'provisional President of Africa', and conferred honours such as 'Duke of Uganda', and 'Knight Commander' and 'Order' of 'the Nile' on those who knelt in front of his throne where he sat robed and ready to dub them with a sword. But there must have been something in his style that appealed to the people. True he was a dreamer, but then Man is a dreamer. Great men simply happen to be having the same dream as their fellow men, at the same time, and in the same place. They recognize and exploit this.

'Africa for the Africans at home and abroad!' this was his

rallying cry. The King of Swaziland once told Mrs Marcus Garvey that he knew the names of only two black men in the West, Jack Johnson the boxer, and Marcus Garvey. And Jomo Kenyatta, the father of independent Kenya, has talked of how in 1921 he and other Kenyan nationalists found inspiration in the words of Garvey's newspaper, *Negro World*. All this and the fact remains that the brother never went to Africa, never spoke any African languages, and never transported a single returnee across the Atlantic.

Question: do you think Joe would have bought shares in the Black Star Steamship Company? I am not sure about this. You might discuss Garvey with him and then bring up the question directly. I would be interested in his answer.

Your brother,

Rudi

Dear Alice,

Thank you for your short note. I also acknowledge the arrival of the Christmas card although, as you know, I do not formally recognize the existence of Christmas as a day of festivity and rejoicing. Not being of the Christian faith this is hardly surprising, but perhaps I would feel less hostile about the day if I were able to use it, as many non-Christians do, as a time when I might take pleasure in the coming together of my family. This, given my present circumstances, is impossible (unless you were all crazy enough to come and spend Christmas down here!). For the last seven Christmasses I have wondered if I will ever again take pleasure in a simple family gathering on 25 December. For me the innocent joy of the day has been destroyed by my years of confinement. However, if this is the only debris I carry with me as I step back towards you then I will have sojourned well.

I have just returned from my half-hour walk. There were fewer faces than usual pressed up to the bars. And up on the thirty-foot watchtowers the pigs seemed half asleep. As the world pivots silently on its axis and orientates itself towards another year there is a feeling of peace. I know tomorrow will be different. But tomorrow is the second day of the year in which you and I will embrace without their watchful porkish eyes boring into us. I am four months away from the main population, and perhaps as many months again away from you. I have plans for us both so hold on.

I have been in receipt of bulletins on your illness from Joe. I did not expect you to have the time or the strength to write so

126

it was an unexpected pleasure. You describe yourself as an invalid. Slow down the word into its two components. In-valid. There is nothing invalid about you. You are a very valid part of our world, but as eventually happens to us all you are now reaching the stage when your senescent body is not capable of obeying your instructions with the panache and speed that it once was. You have made a wise, if not altogether voluntary decision to stop working and stay home in the crib. There will be much for you to look forward to in your new life once Joe and I have pooled our physical and mental resources.

Are you not extremely proud of the way your man has developed in the last year? He is a thinking and hard-working brother who has taken this important step of night classes and submitted himself to the discipline and precision that such a move demands. Automobile maintenance and servicing offers much scope for growth. The death of Popa Williams has made a real leader out of Joe.

Moma, I can write no more because of the brightness of the light. I have tried to persuade the Gestapo Police that I need an eye test, but so far nothing. I spend periods of the day with the wet corner of a sheet soothing and shielding my eyes. I am now learning to see with my ears. I am prepared for anything.

With love, your son,

Rudi

Dear Laverne,

I have just finished my thirty-ninth consecutive cigarette. I am making an effort to keep warm. Do you exercise? I am getting a little flabby where my muscles should be firm and well-toned. The situation is causing me much distress but every time I try to exercise the pigs do what they can to disturb me. I shall have to be more cunning or wait until I am released and then embark upon a major program of physical reconstruction.

I want to look briefly at the lives of a few brothers who are still alive. You have suggested that Paul Robeson is a figure you would like to know more about, and indeed when I looked and analysed his life I found him to be a truly extraordinary man. It is likely – I have already mentioned this – that you have access to more information than myself, but all I can do is to offer up my interpretation of the correct way to read these people's lives and works. In other words, this is an individual revolutionary man's view, which it goes without saying will not be shared by the white man nor by some of our would-be brothers and sisters.

In 1927 Oscar Hammerstein, the Jewish composer, asked Robeson to sing the following lines, 'Niggers all work on de Mississippi, Niggers all work while de white folks play.' Robeson made him change the offensive word to 'Darkies', which might not seem like much today, but dare you imagine how many so-called black men, both then and now, would have gone along with the word 'nigger'? The answer is plenty. Robeson had the presence of mind to stand up straight and speak out clearly and forcibly on anything he believed in. He has always been this way inclined.

Robeson was born in Princeton in 1898, not on campus, because they did not allow blacks there to either study or live. Paul's father, Reverend Bill Robeson, used to hang with the college top man, but when Bill asked him about Bill Junior attending Princeton the college chief tagged Bill with the old color bar. This college fascist was Woodrow Wilson, later to become President of the United States. Young Paul was the real family genius. He won a scholarship to Rutgers (a white school), where he sang, and acted, and played football right up to the level of All-American. Then Paul passed on to Columbia Law School where he studied by day and earned a living as an actor in the evening. He graduated on the eve of the Harlem Renaissance, a six feet six inch, good-looking negro actor, with brains upstairs and the world at his feet. But he had no desire to simply live and die in an American arena; he wanted to travel, and travel can affect the mind in strange but often positive ways.

In Europe Paul earned himself a fine reputation on the boards, then he took off to Russia where they treated him like a king. It was in Russia that he learned for the first time to feel free of the stigma of race. He finally realized how much psychological burden he had been labouring under. Paul got into socialism: he sang on the front line of the Spanish Civil War and closed down the struggle for a day as both sides came to listen. He learned how to sing in German, Chinese, Swahili, Hebrew, Spanish, and Russian, then he set about learning African languages like Yoruba, Efik and Twi. The brother was going back and going deep, but they had him fixed now as both a dangerous black and a dangerous red. The white American man's greatest fear is a black man who knows who he is.

Robeson showed up in 1945 at the Paris Peace Conference and said that America was an imperialistic power and he could not imagine black Americans wanting to fight Soviet troops. He was probably right because among the demobbed brothers there was some serious discontentment. Having got out of a 'Jim Crow' army they were expected to go and sit at the back of the bus again. The American government tried to make a proselyte out of Robeson and buy him off with fat contracts, and when he refused they took his passport, ruined his career and threatened to kill him. They definitely messed with his health (some say they poisoned him) but he has never repented. They rewrote the record books so that the Collegiate All-American football team of 1917–18 had nobody in it named Robeson. They do that stuff in Russia, but they do it in America too. The McCarthy period was not too much different from the Stalinist period in the Soviet Union. I suggest you make a comparative study.

When you hear people talking about Civil Rights what they tend to forget is that Robeson was a father of the movement, although he was far more interested in rooting it in socialism than in Christian morality. Maybe that is why we never see him on the television, or mentioned by the other self-appointed leaders. I wonder if they realize what a debt they owe to this African Renaissance man? Laverne, dig up some contemporary information on Robeson. I think he lives in Pennsylvania.

Your brother,

Rudi

Dear Miss Bailey,

I do not see why you found it necessary to bring a man with you today. Was the purpose of your visit a deliberate attempt to humiliate me? I know nothing of the brother's background, his present occupation, or his future plans. You said his name was Eric: he then sat and stared like a farouche child as we attempted some form of communication. Was he your body-guard? Did you fear for your personal safety if you were to visit with me alone? It is a sick and sad commentary on African womanhood that you are unable to sit casually across a small table and exchange ideas with a brother without harbouring thoughts of rape and potential molestation. In the last hour your philosophy has revealed itself to be that of a reactionary. I offered you companionship in the form of a brother–sister relationship. I offered you much in the way of scope for the development of your political and social ideas. This was not to be single-file traffic, for there is much that I could, and should, have learned from such a beautiful sister. But I fear you are repressed. With you at its helm the 'Rudi Williams Defense Committee' is a sham. Please disband it. Or else step aside and let somebody else take charge. I asked for legal representation, you have done nothing about this. I asked for more details about the group, you have given me little more than abstract generalizations. I fail completely to see what it is that motivates you or people like you. Eric and yourself must find a simpler and more fashionable cause than Rudi Williams. Malcolm once said that the true nature of a woman will surface on her face while dancing. I regret that I had not the opportunity to observe you dancing before the present charade arrived at this sad and regrettable conclusion. You, Miss Bailey, are a source of great disappointment.

Farewell,

Rudolph Leroy Williams

Dear Alice,

Thank you for your letter. I realize it must cause you some distress to write, but I am glad that you manage to do so. I am myself recovering from a damaged arm and will never again take for granted the gift of effortless and free-flowing writing. The physical energy involved in this act is underestimated by those who suffer no disability. I am cold, but the worst is over. I do, however, need eyeglasses and they will cost twenty-five dollars. If Joe could find a way of saving the odd dollar or so then I would be eternally in his debt.

The eye doctor was very good. He confirmed that constant bright light and the excessive reading that I have indulged in have combined to cause this deterioration to my eyesight. The sooner Joe can rustle up the money the better. I have always tried to attenuate the effect these pigs have on my person, but this permanent damage to my health is something I find difficult to come to terms with. I am trying to compose myself and adopt a sanguine frame of mind.

I have discovered that my half-hour walk each day in the courtyard is compulsory. Today I did not wish to go out fearing that my cold might turn to flu and then something worse. But the pigs (there were two of them) positively glowed with joy at the possibility of being able to inflict a legal beating upon me. I walked: I had no desire to knuckle with them. Nothing else is new. I am still writing to Laverne and remain amazed at her grasp of ideas and situations. You must be very proud of her.

There are a few words I wish to address to somebody that you are familiar with. As I do not have any address through

133

which I might contact her I trust you will pass on the following words.

It is now many years since we have spoken and in that time not a day has passed by when I have not thought about you and our child. I do not think about you in the romantic sense that one normally associates with long periods of separation, but you and Femi are a part of my life and I would like to build some form of communication with you. It is important for a girl to know who her father is and through this knowledge gain a firmer grip on the complexities of the world. After all we are born of both seed and egg, and should the child choose to minimize the influence of one or other of these component parts she should at least be exposed to both so that a rational choice might be made. That is all I am asking: that Femi be given the same chance in life as any other child. To know and, if she chooses, to reject her father. G., you have given her no choice at all. For her it is a very untenable position from which to tackle the obstacles that life tosses into our path. I am an older and wiser man whose social circumstances will soon take a very definite turn for the better. I hope that we might come to some arrangement before this turn occurs.

Alice, I want to say as little as possible to you concerning G. except that you make sure my message reaches her. I trust you will do this for me.

Your son,

Rudi

Dear Laverne,

I had expected to hear back from you by now but clearly you must be busy on some project or other. With reference to Phillis Wheatley: I mentioned how the African has always had a sad tendency to be adopted by, and then come to rely upon, the white man. This can be taken to an even further extreme when the African begins to play the fool for the white man, unthinkingly parodying himself and his people in the most grotesque and demeaning caricatures. If this desire to giggle and gawk emanates from an individual of obvious genius then the sense of rage and disappointment among African observers is all the more acute. This is happening in the case of the jazz musician, Louis Armstrong, the man whom they call 'Laughin' Louis'. I do not know what it is (his bank balance aside) that he has to laugh about.

He chicken-struts and plays the darky for the white man. His image is that of a water-melon eating, giggling, sweating, happy-go-lucky, superstitious, mount-anything-that-moves, brainless, helpless, shuffling child. He grins and laughs and calls other brothers 'Shine' and 'Sunshine'. The white man laughs at the negro playing the white-created role of Sambo. It is the only black role that is consistently in vogue because the white man can relate to the psychology and complexity of the character; in other words, none. So why is it that a musical genius, a man with an individual singing voice, a brother who single-handedly changed the shape of twentieth-century music, should so relish the lesser part of Uncle Tom? Every time I see the jackass on television I curl up in anger and embarrassment. I expect they still put him on the television, don't they? On he shuffles or slides, as though he does not know how to walk. Jesus, he has two good legs and a decent pair of shoes on his feet, so what's his problem? He comes shuffling on stage, then looks up as though he's just noticed the audience. His eyes roll around his head like fisheyes, then he grins that big white grin, as wide as a railroad track, and then he starts to giggle and guffaw. Tittle-goddamn-tattle, playing the child they so desperately want him to be. Then he picks up his horn, mops down his obligatory sweaty face, and starts to blow. He blows sweeter than anybody has ever blown a horn. Then he starts to mop his brow again and giggle and strut and roll his eyes at the audience and scat and get all ugly in his Uncle Thomas face. Oh my God, why does the brother do this? Louis Armstrong, the greatest of them all, the man without whom there might possibly have been no jazz as we know it today, why? Maybe it has something to do with his growing up in twenties America? Back then the minstrel show had just been replaced by the vaudeville coon shows, which contained sketches of black men attacking each other with razors, eating chicken, pork chops, and water-melons, indulging in voodoo, rapping about red-hot mommas and never-too-faithful poppas, and everybody doing a little smoke and talking bull. This was what America expected, and still expects, of the black man: and Louis Armstrong loves applause, and wants to please, so he does it. Perhaps it's as simple as this? His repertoire has included songs called, 'Shine', 'Snowball' and 'Shoe Shine Boy'; he does not appear to have developed a sense of decorum. It is on record that his manager (he always puts his affairs into the hands of a white man) once told him: 'Play for the public. Sing and play and smile. Smile, goddam-mit, smile. Give it to them.' And like the good slave, Louis will sing for his master and run through his eye-rolling, dice-rolling, tambourine-banging, yassuh, forelock-tugging, knee-scraping, nauseating performance. His music is tolerable only with one's eyes closed.

Last I heard of Armstrong he was still doing this same act.

And this in an age of Malcolm's death, Emmett Till, Luther
King, and Civil Rights. Armstrong needs an ass-whupping.
  Your brother,

                                                  Rudi

Dear Alice,

Thank you for your short letter. I use the term 'short' as an adjective, not in a judgemental sense. I am pleased to receive communication from you irrespective of length. Your words always help to soothe the difficulties of my present condition. I must, however, say straight up that I am disappointed that you have made no response to my enclosure for G. You do not admit that you know her whereabouts, or hint as to whether or not you have passed on my words. Perhaps you have condemned them to the trash can? I think a little of your Christian kindness would have been in order here as it causes my soul some anguish to linger in the dark when it is clear there is no need for me to do so. Please rectify your error as soon as possible.

Have you read the works of Richard Wright? I think you should, particularly *Black Boy*, a book about his childhood in Mississippi. He is a much misunderstood man due to the fact that he flirted a little with Communism. In this sense I too am a much misunderstood man. He wrote a book entitled *The Outsider*. Could you please ask Joe to make inquiries about the purchase of this book. And another book (by the same R. Wright) entitled *Black Power*. Wright coined what has now become a familiar African–American phrase for rebellion. Laverne should have copies of some of his works: if not I will give what I have to Joe when he next visits. You really should study him. The sagacity of his mind is overpowering for a literary man.

Is Joe working so hard that he is unable to find the time to write? I assume that this is the case, and naturally I am not making a complaint of any kind. It is simply a question. How much more of his course is there to run? I do not even know if it is a full year's program or just a semester. My filing system is in my head, but sometimes I forget things. Perhaps you might ask him if it is alright for me to write, even though he may not be able to reply. He may say 'no', for often a man feels compelled to reply to a letter even if he has not the time. I do not wish to cause any confusion in Joe's mind. He must maintain clarity of purpose.

Thank you for the twenty-five dollars, which has now been converted into a pair of plain-looking – I speak now of fashion – but highly functional eyeglasses. They have made an enormous difference to my visual powers and have led me to wonder how it is I ever managed without them.

Life in this dystopia goes on. The practise of hurling human waste into my cell has begun again. The pigs seem intent upon making this last two months of thraldom as hellish as possible. They wish to provoke me into some action that will result in my being detained here, but they will not succeed. I cannot imagine another day in this place beyond April. I would literally go mad were I to have to return here. I am the only captive in this part of the camp. I am a special exhibit they are now frightened to lose. Any chance of holding on to me for a little longer will be eagerly seized. Their moral turpitude knows no depths.

I am sorry to hear about Aunt Sophie's stroke. I have always been touched by how close you are to both Bea and Sophie. You form a sisterly triangle of great warmth.

Your son,

Rudi

Dear Laverne,

I shall briefly outline the life and character of Richard Wright (1908–60). He was born in Natchez, Mississippi. He grew up 'Jim Crow' and not understanding the white man, fearing him, but wanting to be like him in terms of privileges. He would never escape this conundrum. You can take a brother out of the south, but you can never take the south out of the brother.

He was basically self-educated. He travelled north to Chicago and began to write. In 1940 he published his first novel, *Native Son*. Within three weeks he had sold a quarter of a million copies. Five years later he published *Black Boy*. This book sold half a million copies in five months. He married a Jewess named Ellen, who gave her parents the finger because they didn't like the fact that she was hanging out with a 'nigger'. They moved to France because of racial problems. In his journal, Wright wrote, 'Can a negro ever live like a man in America?' The answer was clear to him. While emigrating to France, on board the *SS United States*, his wife was insulted for being with a 'nigger'. For a while the French treated him like royalty. But Wright should have gone and settled back in Africa if he was intent upon living outside of America in a country free from racial strife. When the novelty of French residence wore off, and the money ran out, he started to worry. Eventually he died of a stress-induced heart attack in Paris. Wright has the ability to momentarily ameliorate the world with the clarity of his vision. He is outstanding.

There is little more I can say that will make any sense for

I am not sure if you have read the man. Remember I asked you to read Wright and formulate your own assessment of his life and character. You have failed to do so. There is much to discuss about Wright, his involvement with the Communist Party, the CIA campaign against him, his association with Nkrumah, Sartre, and others, but I am loath to pursue these topics until you reconfirm that we are engaged in a dialogue. I trust all is well with you?

Your brother,

Rudi

March 1968

Dear Laverne,

I have found an essay by Richard Wright entitled 'Joe Louis uncovers dynamite'. The essay itself is dynamite. Muhammed Ali has always been my main man. Tell me, how is the brother doing? He is one of our great African–American heroes, somebody on whom the younger generation of males should seriously consider modelling their lives. However, what I underestimated was the influence of Joe Louis on the lives of our people only one generation ago. According to Wright, after Joe whupped Jim Braddock, and took the title, every black man in America was able to walk down the street and look Mr Charlie in the face and say, 'Yeah my man, something bothering you?' I also read about how in one of these Southern states they changed their method of killing people – which usually means African people – from the gallows to the gas chamber. When they wanted to check out how humane this was they put a microphone into the chamber to record what the victim's last words were. As chance would have it the first man up just happened to be a brother: his last words were, 'Save me, Joe Louis. Save me, Joe Louis. Save me, Joe Louis . . .'

An Alabama boy, Joe took the title in June 1937 and, according to Wright, that night over 100,000 people spilt out on to the streets of Harlem, drums going, car horns and cow bells ringing out, all kinds of celebrating going on. When war came Joe joined the army, had a couple of fights and donated his purses to the Army and Navy Relief Funds. He retired in 1947 having made over four and a half million dollars in the ring, but he was broke. Yeah, broke. And he owed over a million dollars in back taxes. The government even charged him tax on the money he donated to the relief funds! He'd lived high and fast, but he had also been ripped off by the mendacious white boys who were running him. As soon as he was broke they split. Today he still owes the tax man more money than they got stashed away in Fort Knox. I am not trying to absolve him of blame, but he means something to our community. We should not allow a man who means so much to languish so low. What of these black millionaires? Have they moved directly from a state of ethnological colonialism to unashamed dollarism? Why do they not rally around and put something back into our community: like pride and self-respect. We should look after Joe. This paragon of pugilistic excellence is worthy of our support.

There has always been a debate about whether we African people in America should play sports at all. My position is clear. We should play sports for recreational, physical and financial purposes. But we must not do so at the cost of underdeveloping our mental, intellectual, or business faculties.

I had no intention of including another sketch as I suspect you are tiring of our communication. However, I just happened to stumble across a perfect link between Wright and Joe Louis. Is it not possible for you to write to me? Is Joe afflicted with the same disease as yourself? I do not understand why one of you is not able to write. Is your mutual silence an accident or is it occurring by design?

Your brother,

Rudi

Dear Alice,

So Gwendolyn is a nurse and she is married. You did not say
to whom she is married, what his status is, or if he is able to
provide properly for her and Femi. (I beg you to please not use
the name Sondra to me. I called my child Femi.) I cannot
pretend that it does not cause me great hurt to know that Femi
thinks this man is her father. Why this deception? Surely she
will eventually find out and come to hate the man for his
duplicity and love me for my innocence and suffering. Has
Gwendolyn some mental problems that she cannot understand
this? Femi is nearly eight now – am I right? Soon she will be old
enough to start communicating with her father. I refuse to take
a back seat in her life and hand over the wheel to some New
Jersey faggot. I was man enough to sire her and I am man
enough to hunt and provide for her needs, to clothe her in
winter, to feed and protect her in the summer months. Moma,
I require you to find out their daily movements. Upon my
release I will take a bus to New Jersey where I shall recapture
what is rightfully mine. Please do not be alarmed, I am merely
doing what is correct according to natural law. If I did not feel
so deeply attached to my own flesh and blood you would accuse
me of being selfish and possessing an uncaring spirit. Well, I
am neither selfish nor uncaring, and I intend to prove it. I am
sure that in law Gwendolyn should have notified me of her
intention to spirit away my child into the tangle of her marriage. I am requesting you to find out if I am correct on this
point. I also wish you to inform me why you have not
told the child the truth about me? I cannot imagine that you

would search out your grandchild, yet forget the loyalty you owe to your own son. What of Gwendolyn's mother? She always seemed close to you. Did she not object to Gwendolyn's behavior? The situation is intolerable. I have every intention of rectifying it the moment I step beyond Belsen. My time is now calibrated in days and weeks, not months. It will not be long. These are testing times. I have to conduct myself with the severest discipline. One wrong move and I may be forced to remain here, a situation I do not believe an ordinary human being could endure for another year. Let us hope. Now that I have the incentive of Femi to add to my political ideals, and my desire to be with you, I think I am sufficiently motivated to tackle this fast-approaching hurdle with confidence. Take care of yourself. I will hear from you when you are able.

Your son,

Rudi

Dear Miss Lucilla Hodges,

You say you are a lawyer. Let me be more precise; you describe yourself as an attorney. What do you truly know about the circumstances of my case? Are you familiar with the conditions in which I attempt to survive? It seems as though they want me to serve natural life for attempting to steal forty dollars. Do you know this? Do you know how long I have languished in this zoo within a zoo known as Max Row? Has anybody ever curve-balled a lump of human excrement into your florally decorated bedroom? I no longer speak to, nor have any communication with, any members of the 'Rudi Williams Defense Committee'. You say they 'put you on to me'. You also claim that you are acting independently of them. Either you are with them or against them – now which is it? I am about to be released into a wider, but equally secure captivity. You write me as the game goes into overtime. If you wish to act as my lawyer you will have to understand three things.

(1) I have neither money nor assets.

(2) I will not break. My position is not negotiable.

(3) To them I am a symbol of something they must destroy.

The battle-lines are drawn, the troops massed, the guerrilla war will be protracted. If we are to continue our communication I must know about your past cases and your success rate. I must know your thoughts on how our struggle might proceed in this alien American society. I must know who you read for relaxation and who for study. Before you ingress any further these questions must be answered.

Until the morrow,

R. L. Williams

Dear Joe,

I want you to be the first to know that I have made it back upstairs to the main population. The vicissitudes of my life defy prediction. I can have darkness. My eyes can rest easy at night. There is the company of other captives, although most are reactionary in their behavior and attitudes. There are newspapers – tenth-hand, torn and smudged by the time they reach me – but newspapers all the same. I can walk about in the day for a half-hour or five hours, whatever I please. Restrictions still apply, but to me they are as welcome and as liberal as the emancipation proclamation that we have yet to hear.

The company of men is the strangest of the phenomena that I must adjust to. How to talk to them, when to listen, how to remain calm. Life in the main body of the camp is centred on action, not meditation. As a result I find that while I have developed mentally, and become a person who operates from a broader and more reflective base, the young bloods in this part of the camp are still concerned with mirroring the daily pattern of the unthinking lives they led beyond the gates. There is therefore much profane language and talk about 'sticking' pigs and pale cons if they should step out of line. There is also much internal brother-on-brother violence, born largely of frustration, but no more justifiable because of this. All it serves to do is to entertain those who see it as comically inevitable that 'niggers' cannot behave even among themselves. I have to continually remind myself of the truth that inside every brother is a potential revolutionary, but it is often difficult to

147

be so generous with those who it would appear are making a conscious effort to be uncivilized.

There is one remarkable, but arcane, man whose acquaintance I have made. A dark Cuban brother, perhaps a shade closer to Africa than either you or I. He wants to go back to Cuba; he feels that he has made a mistake fleeing Castro's revolutionary state. His family owned much property in Havana and it seemed the natural thing to do, but they have not flourished in Florida. Unable to control his libido he is serving ten years for rape, a crime I have no sympathy with. He explained to me that it was not rape, that the American girl was dishonoring him so he had little choice but to show his mastery and take his trim at knife-point, but I still have no sympathy for him. If we behave like animals then we deserve to be viewed and treated as such. Can you think of a more disquieting crime?

Joe, for the first time in eight years I feel as though I am heading in the right direction. I feel as though I am close to discovering a panacea for all my previous ailments. The parole board meets in October, some six months hence. All I have to do is keep out of trouble and I should be with you all by Christmas. I am even thinking of taking up a voluntary job, cleaning the block or doing some gardening. Anything that will help rebuild me physically and assist my good-conduct record. My arm is still painful and I suspect a little arthritic. Damp may have gotten into it where they set the bone awkwardly. I will need a good doctor upon my release. He may find it necessary to break the arm again and re-set it. I hope not, but I want to be a whole man for you, Alice, Laverne and Femi. A twenty-seven-year-old man should be able to support his family in full health.

Yours,

Rudi

Dear Joe,

So they finally got King. It was inevitable that he would become a martyr, but was there ever such a violent commotion in these United States of America after the death of a white man? What does that tell you about our historical position? It tells you that we are underdeveloped and perhaps rely too heavily upon one person to lead us, like sheep, across the Rubicon. And when that person is taken from us (which he surely will be, for he is mortal flesh and blood and likely to be courageous and say things that the white man does not want to hear) we are numbed into shock and then stung into blind and motiveless violence. If we could learn to find leadership in ourselves, and acquire a sense of individual purpose, then we might get the death of Dr King into its proper perspective.

He was a fine orator, perhaps the finest this land has ever hosted. That he should belong to us is a cause for great pride. He was also a fine writer. Have you read his books? If not you must do so, for he wielded a pen with the same sense of authority that he wielded the sword of justice. His disquisitions were both pellucid and powerful. He was also a fine family man, the father of four beautiful children, and a loving and devoted husband to an intelligent and pretty sister. These are great and sound qualities that most of us aspire to but never reach. However, it is in the area of his Christian philosophy, and the application of this philosophy to the struggle with the white man, that he and I differ.

I am not a Christian, and I have never read the Bible, but if a book tells me that a man who slaps me upside the head must go unslapped in return, and furthermore I must love this man, then the book is way out of line. It is not in human nature to behave in such a manner. Do you know of any animal in the whole universe that is a pacifist? Does the buck deer, having been savaged near to death by the panther, want to forgive the panther and perhaps talk about it? I doubt this very much. We must learn to deal with the man *before* the man deals with us. King and his people spent far too much time marching, getting beat up, talking, getting beat up again, and then pummelled into jail. King claimed his pacifism was intended to provoke the conscience of the American white man. Why, I wonder, does he imagine that the American white man has a conscience? If his proposed course of action could be deemed to have been even partially successful then there would have been no cheering and partying among the pigs and white captives on the news of his death. For them, King's murder heralded a time for joy and celebration. A head 'nigger' was dead. No need to bruise our knuckles on that one any more.

I am deeply saddened by what has happened to Dr King, but would like to make it clear that his demise is of no real importance: his life is what matters. He was no showcase nigger, although there were those close to him who might best be described as pharisaical attendants and bootlickers. Perhaps we should use Dr King's death as the signal for looking deeper into ourselves and finding a more self-reliant form of leadership. It is a defeatist strategy to pin our hopes on any one man.

Your son,

Rudi

Dear Laverne,

Still nothing from either you or Joe despite the fact that one of our most revered brothers was shot down by a lone white K K K-er. Do you have nothing to say on the matter? I had half-expected some note of congratulations from at least one of you on my reaching back to the comparative sanity of the main camp block, but again nothing. In times past I would have suspected Alice of poisoning your minds against me, but Alice has developed into a fine and capable woman who I believe has the right attitude to face whatever difficulties life might now provide her with. She has quit slaving for the white women who ruined her health in their kitchens and their bathrooms, on their floors and in their laundry rooms. I do not believe she would discourage you from communication with me so I can only imagine that this is some decision you have taken independently.

I assume that Dr King's death has touched you in some way. In my case it has made me reflect not only upon Dr King, but upon our other 'leader', Malcolm X, whom we lost only three years ago. Did you know that Malcolm was born out west in Omaha, Nebraska, and that as a child white men came and lynched his father, leaving his mother to bring up a sizeable family all by herself. And imagine it used to upset white Americans when he would speak of them in less than complimentary terms! For a while he dealt dope for Basie and Ellington, he packed a gun, shone shoes, then wound up in jail, all of this before he was my age! And then he discovered Allah and it changed his life. He travelled back to Africa, met his people, and came to realize much about himself and the world. It was then that other blacks – I will not dignify them with the name Africans – had him killed in a pique of jealous rage.

Dr King and Malcolm will live on as different sides of the same coin, the one we African people are spending in an attempt to make the American white man change his ways. Are we receiving any change? I do not think so. Garvey-ism, a new and modern phase of it, is what we must look for now. Today's Black Star Steamship Company will be an airline. But we must go as individuals and not rally behind a single leader, for America will break that man, as she has done all the others. Perhaps in time she will break me, but not without a struggle of the most operatic proportions.

A final point in this obituary note. Listen to what Malcolm had to say about himself in relation to Dr King.

> The goal has always been the same . . . in the racial climate of this country today, it is anybody's guess which of the 'extremes' in approach to the black man's problems might personally meet a fatal catastrophe first – 'non-violent' Dr King, or so-called 'violent' me.

If only their supporters had asked for a moratorium on supposed ideological conflict so these two great leaders could have put their heads together. If only . . .

Laverne, these are our people who are falling like bowling pins. Can you not organize among your friends and acquaintances out there and help raise individual consciousness otherwise this tragic and seemingly inveterate cycle will never be broken.

Your brother,

Rudi

May 1968

Dear Laverne,

I have been reading the newspapers and slowly catching up on what was happening in the world while I spent time downstairs. I am very disturbed that nobody informed me about Nkrumah's being deposed. Nobody mentioned the Chinese Cultural Revolution. That there were racial riots in Florida last year went unreported in your letters, and what of Vietnam! Do you realize how many brothers are fighting over there in this pointless and reactionary war? Sixteen per cent of their army is African.

This evening we had a very ugly scene in the television room. For reasons still unclear to me the pigs decided to project a film. I assume they thought it a special treat, much as you would hand out candy to children. We captives filed in and took up our seats, whites and Mexicans to one side, blacks to the other, and we waited. The movie turned out to be the latest Sidney Poitier vehicle (although for me his wheels have never turned). It was entitled *Guess Who's Coming to Dinner*. You are probably familiar with this celluloid junk, as I understand it achieved something of a minor success when released on the street last year. Have you seen the movie? If so do you really swallow that Sidney Poitier had so many qualifications? For me the movie ended at the point Spencer Tracey picked up the telephone to check out this 'Sambo' who was troubling his pasty-white daughter. Poitier's supposed earned degrees and commendations began to sound like a shopping-list. Spencer Tracey put down the phone. We had us a 'super-nigger'. He wasn't like those others, but still he wasn't good enough.

153

This film had nothing to do with the lives of African people, past, present, and I imagine future. The brothers hated it, the whites hated it, the pigs hated it. It was the first time we have all agreed on anything. We, the camp-dwellers, exist in a world of reality and you cannot fool anybody in here. We know when something stinks of artifice. However, we did not like the fact that we all agreed. A few brothers started throwing insults and before you could blink there was a riot alarm.

Nothing happened. I am back in my cell but cannot free my mind of the poison that is *Guess Who's Coming to Dinner*. It is so far removed from the realities of the known world that I would not permit my dog to view it.

Laverne, this will be my final letter to you. Over the past months I have sung to you a little cargo rap about the children of Africa who arrived in this country by crossing the water: Crispus, Phillis, Toussaint, Harriet, Marcus, Louis, Paul, Richard, Joe, even Malcolm and Dr King. Perhaps you have lost your singing voice and can no longer perform harmonies with me. Just remember this; they have called us nigger, then negro, then colored, and now black; do you imagine they will ever call us Americans? Surely it makes sense to walk tall and free as an African? If you remember nothing else of our dialogue then remember this. I am sorry that my tutelary role has ended so sadly and prematurely. Farewell.

Your brother,

Rudi

May 1968

Dear Miss Lucilla Hodges,

Your letter is vague. I appreciate your congratulations. I think I have earned them over the last year, but I am disturbed about the lack of information concerning yourself. I asked you to supply me with some biographical details, some material on your career to date, and your analysis of my case. In plain terms I go before the parole board in October. If you can assist then fine. If you feel that the presence of an attorney might be a hindrance then you must let me know. But before any of this can be discussed I need to know about *you*. You do not seem to understand that I cannot be expected to place my affairs in the hands of a reactionary. I must be vigilant. I am ever alert and listening for the other shoe to fall. My life depends upon it. You might at least begin with a photograph.

Sincerely,

Rudi Williams

Dear Alice,

Thank you for your visit. I was overjoyed that I could once again be in your presence and hold your hands in mine. You looked tired and unwell, Alice. I think you should either consult another doctor or go back to the one who is treating you and demand from him a second opinion. Often a doctor makes the wrong analysis, although they are understandably loath to ever admit this. I wish for nothing more than to be close to you and have you once again returned to full and blooming health. You deserve this, and more, as repayment for the strains and stresses of the life you have had to endure. In future I would like to know as far in advance as possible when I might see you again. A surprise visit is pleasant, but if I know when you are coming then it will be possible for me to do more than stare back lovingly into your eyes. I am sorry if I was a little mute, but the unexpected nature of your visit, plus the news that you delivered, shook me up.

So Joe has taken George into the house and given up his night-school studies? His painfully acquired notion of scholarship is to be mortgaged in exchange for what? You were very generous, Alice, in suggesting that this might possibly be the reason he has not been in touch. This is precisely the reason for his silence; he knows he has done everything I have advised him not to do, and in a cowardly way he has not the strength of mind to defend himself like a man and argue a case to back up his actions. So he remains silent. I thought Joe was finally stepping out from behind his slave mask and adopting the manner, features, and attitudes of a fully grown man. I was wrong. How can he have lived in excess of half-a-century on this planet yet still conduct himself as though he were a child? Malcolm was correct when he suggested that we did not land on Plymouth Rock, it landed on us. Joe is one of those who has allowed himself to be crushed. I have finished with him as both a father and as a man. Please do not mention his name to me again.

The case of Laverne is more serious. I half-expected Joe to fall from grace. However, I expected Laverne to grow from year to year into a beautiful revolutionary sister. I have made a terrible error. I imagine that being a mother yourself the shock is even greater for you. Do you know the boy or man who has done this thing to her? You seemed barely able to raise your voice above a whisper when the time came to deal with Laverne's disgrace. Does this boy want to marry her? Where did she find the privacy so that he might have access to her body? You and I, Moma, have much in common. There is a deep visceral bond between us. Your husband and daughter have disappointed us both, but we will go on. Hold on, only five more months.

Your son,

Rudi

Dear Lucy,

(You say this is the soubriquet by which I must address you). I see now your reluctance to furnish me with more biographical data. I do not blame you for what or who you are, I blame the so-called Rudi Williams 'Defense Committee', the stupidity of whom is now compounded by what I can only assume to be malice.

The situation is laughable and I hope that you are able to smile about it. You seem a decent enough person and, glancing at your biographical data, you are clearly a thoroughbred professional. You are something of a legal high-flyer. Congratulations.

You claim to be interested in my case because you have minority interests 'at heart'. In which part of your heart does your interest in 'minorities' reside? Or do you wear your interest badge-like on your sleeve in the hope that others might admire and look upon you as the contemporary American 'Good Samaritan'? Do you have 'minority' blood coursing through your veins? How dare you refer to any blackman as a minority! In a global context we far outnumber those of the Caucasian ethnological group. Lucy, perhaps you are confused?

What do your parents think of your sacrifice? I assume that to work for an imprisoned blackman who has no money, no material assets, and no viable means of earning or acquiring either (legally, at least), would represent to them a sacrifice, or at best a questionable investment of their daughter's time. Do you hide from them your interest in this area, or have you seized the bull by the nuts and purchased for yourself a black-man as a companion? If so, do you display him?

My dear Miss Ann, I have seen too much and done too little to be caught up in a Tokenism-bag at this stage. Why do you not use your skills to apprehend and prosecute the killers of Medger Evers? Is it five years now? The crime remains 'un-solved'. Or you might more profitably defend the young people who shout, 'LBJ! LBJ! How many kids did you kill today!' These rich college kids are in need of your talents (and they have money). You see, there is much I have to achieve with this life of mine, and I have no choice but to adopt a position of deep suspicion towards those who would latch on to my shirt-tail. If you want a ride, you ride on my shoulders, with my permission, and I will carry you as far as I choose and dispose of you safely by the side of the road when I am good and ready. But before I stoop to scoop you up I need to know why you wish to ride with me. Having minority interests 'at heart' is not good enough.

Sincerely,

Rudi Williams

Laverne,

I received your letter this morning. It is now 8 p.m. and I finally feel composed enough to formulate a reply. Emotional stability is something I have always struggled to acquire, but I am now coming to believe that it is an ideal that lies just beyond man's grasp. We are destined to be for ever tossed about from one high to another low, and we have no means by which we might either arrest the movement or determine the direction in which our emotions ebb and flow.

You claim that the man who bulled you wants also to marry you. You mention this as though it is a small triumph of some kind. The real triumph is his. When he whistled, 'Hey baby, you feel like coming back to my place for breakfast?', and you grinned and followed him like an adulterous dog and let him pile you, he triumphed. You may yet end up modelling on street corners, or as a black fag-hag with uncombed hair and desperate eyes. I did not want this for my sister, but then I wonder if you truly are blood to me. For a spasm of pleasure you have lost the world. Masturbation would have been a more logical way to ease off your frustrations. Your mind and body would now be clean.

If the child is a girl you say you will call it Harriet Phillis. If it is a boy, Malcolm Rudolph. Please do not give my name to your child. You have transformed my soul into a battleground: on the one side there is my innate faith in our people; on the other side is the external evidence of our degradation. Why do you behave like them? Our standards must be different, must be higher. We cannot allow ourselves to be cheapened through

160

submission to animalistic instincts. Goddamn, Laverne, you are my sister. Do you not understand the physical and mental sacrifices I have made in order to reach my current station in life? It may be a low position to you, but inside of me I cannot get any higher without busting out of the top of my head. I am full and whole, and I am proud of you, damn you! I would have moved heaven and earth to do anything for you – you were my sister and my woman. Whatever I have to share you could have taken a piece too. I felt very attached to you in a delicate way. How can I free the 'nigger' in your head? Do I have to bust a hole in your skull? At the moment we have nothing further to say to each other.

Goodbye.

Rudi

Dear Alice,

I am once again down here on Max Row. I apologize to you for the disappointment that this will no doubt cause you. Believe me it is no greater than the pain it is causing me. They inform me that I must survive twelve more months of hell. I do not know if this will be possible. I am, for the first time, truly at the end of my patience. There is nothing left in my batteries – God knows what sources of energy I am now drawing upon. For our people the move from south to north was from outhouses and kerosene lamps to inside toilets and electric lights. Do you remember when I spoke with you on this subject? Well again I must familiarize myself with outhouses and kerosene lamps. Such is the magnitude of my decline and fall.

They shot the younger of the Kennedy brothers. This provoked an ugly situation in the main block and a fight broke out between the white and black captives. I will not deny that I was involved, but I was not the only one. There were maybe fifty or sixty people slugging it out with chairs, tables, anything they could lay their hands on, everybody putting the wood on everybody else. There are now four of us on ice, and all of us are of African origin. Their Gestapo-mentality is clear.

I have concussion and periodically black out. I am still spitting blood and have lost five or six teeth. More importantly I have lost my chance of seeing you and holding you in my arms for over another year. Truly this is too much to bear. Inside I am burning. I have never before asked this of you, but is there not some way in which you might help? Is there nobody to whom you might go and explain my situation? Were any of the white women you slaved for married to judges or high-ranking officials? I am the victim of an injustice that I do not believe the judicial system of any other nation on the face of the earth would tolerate. I will even consider being released into the army and going to Vietnam. Does this not illustrate to you the desperation of my condition? Twenty-three and a half hours of brightness, Moma. I am sure my eyes will deteriorate and that I shall emerge from this camp a blind man.

All politics, revolutionary or otherwise, to one side, I am making a humanistic appeal to whomsoever it might concern. In the bosom of this country there is a man who is being stretched and tortured for forty dollars. Enough is enough. Moma, I do not want to resort to violence, but if I have to go at least one of them will go with me. Am I making myself clear?

Your loving son,

Rudi

June 1968

Dear Lucy,

So they shot your leader: you, the people that think Elvis Presley is funky, and that dancing the twist constitutes a physical revolution. Should I feel sorry? I am not a spiteful man. When they shot his elder brother, Malcolm described it as 'chickens coming home to roost'. This comment led directly to Malcolm's death at the hands of traitors of my own complexion. Now a man – is he white? – has shot a second Kennedy. The country is in a sorry state and I fear there is much worse to come. Who will now dare to run for public office, open their mouths to speak against injustice, or make a stand out there in front of the madding crowd? Will everybody now cower at the prospect of the assassin's bullet? I have lived in daily dread of the bullet for more years than I care to remember. Perhaps others will understand me better as a result of this death.

So here I am in the bowels of this camp, clinging by my fingernails to a fast-receding vision of manumission. Am I making sense? You say you want to help me, you the minority-lover. Well help me now. Get me out of this place. Nothing short of my total and unconditional release will be construed as constituting your having successfully helped me. I do not believe you require anything more than an unfortunate pen-pal with whom you might communicate in order to make you feel even more privileged than you already are. Do you discuss me with your dinner guests? Do you have newspaper clippings of my case? Do you say there are no jobs for blacks, and blacks cannot make the rent? Do you mention white cops, foreign aid and sip wine? Or do you introduce the idea that Mr Charlie doesn't recognize Rudi or Rudi's without a mop in their hand; that if he happens across a brief-cased one a lump forms in his throat and he panics a little as though he has witnessed an apparition? Do your guests whisper to each other about 'the white man's nightmare' – a nigger with a book – and then sip more wine?

Miss Hodges, either act or get out of my life and stay out of it. Your whining does nothing but compound my sense of misery. What time I have left must not be wasted pursuing relationships that are heading in no particular direction. The noose is tightening, action is everything, I no longer have time for discussion. I want you to take a desk lamp and shine it into your face. Try to relax, think, act, concentrate, do everything in this position for twenty-four hours. Is there yet a summary of Che Guevara's life in book form? If so you might mail this to me.

Sincerely,

Rudi

July 1968

Dear Lucy,

This morning I received a letter from my father, Joseph Adolphus Williams. He informs me, in his casual way, that my mother, Alice Delores Williams, passed away three days ago. My father had neither the presence of mind to telephone the prison authorities so that they could immediately inform me, nor had he the common sense to climb on to a bus, ride a train, or steal a car and get his slavish mind and body down here so that he might have the decency to tell her only son to his face. If there was some way in which the cancer in Moma's body might have been transplanted into his, I would have gladly paid to have initiated such an operation. I no longer have any books or materials to study from. But when I was blessed with such luxuries a poster of an African woman for sale, with her five children, used to cause my heart to swell with indignation. Surely the man who fathered these children should have killed any white man who tried to separate the family. If only three or four black men had found the courage to act then our family unit might have remained secure and a resultant sense of responsibility would have been fused into the souls of our men.

Joseph Adolphus Williams is a nigger. He did not deserve somebody as beautiful as Alice. Her life is spent. The two loose ends tied up, made secure, and now tossed to one side. Thank God we die only once. Between myself and eternity there stands nobody. Only my daughter, Femi. Her mother denies my existence and I have never set eyes upon her. Perhaps it is better that I do not mark her. Her new 'father' may have a less troubled soul. He may be a doctor or teacher, somebody who is able to provide for her and ensure that she might live without the scars and bumps and bruises on her fingers and on her knees that Alice collected as a result of her slavery in this America. Between my head and the sky much is possible. I want to disturb the pigs, I want everything to come out past my teeth and tongue and to smash against the wall: I crane back my head and open my mouth. I spread my fingers wide and pump out my arms on either side, and I try to force it but nothing comes, Miss Hodges, and I start to cry like a child and I feel ashamed because I cannot help myself.

Rudolph Leroy Williams

Brothers and Sisters

Are we still looking for black supermen? I have spent nearly eight years of my life (I am now twenty-seven) in prison – that is damn near to a third of my present lifespan. I have yet to find any black supermen. I am the nearest to such a model that I have ever stumbled across. Yet I am no superman.

The ofay pigs grunt and snort and squeal louder with the passing of each day. They are excited now for I have fallen on one knee and they imagine that soon the other knee will buckle and I will holler for mercy. I am tired. Even Ali never fought past fifteen three-minute rounds. Eight years is the bout for the title of all titles, and my Moma just threw in the towel. I picked it up and there's a message sewed into its fabric. It says, 'Be kind to your kinfolk and those who care for you. They may know something you don't know, or have suffered something you have yet to suffer. Be kind!'

I have never been an advocate of Dr King's Christian philosophy. (Rabbis don't drive Cadillacs, they walk. Too many black preachers drive Cadillacs and wear gold rings. They lead nobody except their nasty selves.) However, as I sit here three words of Dr King's flood back into my mind. (I no longer sleep. I have not slept for two weeks. My physical condition is lamentable. My body is atrophying.) Dr King used the phrase as the title of one of his books: 'Strength to Love'. I have not the strength. I do not even have the strength to be kind. Alice, my Moma, she knew this but she did not abandon me. I am strong in theory, in self-discipline, in ability, but I have not learned how to marry these virtues with another type of strength. It involves, I imagine, giving up not acquiring, opening doors not closing them, reaching out not holding back. I am not made of this material. Were I ten years younger, and knowing what I know now, I might have made the effort to acquire such skills. But I am too practised in my own particular patterns of existential behavior. They have served me well and made me a black semi-superman.

I can hear the pigs grunting. Brothers and Sisters, are we familiar with the Jamaican poet, Claude McKay? We should be.

> *If we must die, let it not be like hogs*
> *Hunted and penned in an inglorious spot,*
> *While round us bark the mad and hungry dogs,*
> *Making their mark at our accursed lot.*

And so on.

Remember this is America. This is 1968. This is a country in which two hundred million walk around with their eyes closed. Who won the World Series? Did the Celtics beat the Lakers? Will it be Nixon this time? Do you want mustard with your hot dog? Flowers for your hair? Or bullets for your gun?

Dear Lucy,

Why did you visit me? You claimed to be 'bent out of shape' by my attitude. Why? You offered me no release date. I have made it perfectly clear to you that the only practical purpose of my developing a communicative relationship with you is if it revolves around action. Remember, you cannot attack slavery with moral theory any more than you can pick cotton with words. Liberalism is nothing more than perfumed oppression and I sincerely hope you are not a subscriber. If so the price of our friendship will be subject to inflatory pressures that will drive it beyond the range of your pocket.

I am sorry that you could not disguise your shock on observing my physical condition. At least I was clean and did not trouble your olfactory organs. Once upon a time I might have been mistaken for a two-hundred-pound running back. Who knows, we might even have developed a love-project in different circumstances. Such are the vagaries of life. I am not small-minded enough to hate white people simply because of their lack of color. In your own way you're a fox, do you know that? Yes, swallow deeply. Keep swallowing. Now you are learning.

Rudi Williams

Lucy,

Thank you for your poem. I was not aware the lawyers could write creatively. Today I have been called a 'nigger' forty-six times. There will be a forty-seventh but I do not sit and anticipate its arrival. Do you not understand that when they run the 'stars and stripes' up a flagpole they are obscuring the sun? When they play 'The Star-Spangled Banner' they are blocking out the natural sounds of nature, of birds singing, of the wind rustling through the trees. Were you something other than what you are things might well be different. However, I cannot at this stage run with you. You are kind and warmer than the sun, but you endanger my person. I worry that what I feel in my soul you feel only in your head. Is this true? Go home and call your cracker old man 'Honky' and see how that feels in your soul. Am I getting through to you? Lucy, you'd be guilty by 'sociological association', then maybe one day by 'biological association'. And what happens when you tire of bearing a burdened soul? You split, right? Hell, nobody likes to feel tortured: I don't see why you should want to voluntarily shackle yourself to such a life in the USA (Union of South Africa). It makes no sense. Take care of yourself.

Rudi

Dear Moma,

The overseer has a horse named 'Ginger'. The plantation is wide and stretches beyond the horizon. The days are hard and long. We toil from 'can't see' in the morning to 'can't see' at night. The master is cruel, but nobody 'knows' him better than his slaves. There is strength in this. I have had to learn a new language so forgive me if I make errors while attempting to temporarily reclaim our own. How are the crops? Have the rains come? Father and sister, are they safe? Thirty feet above me a man sits on a watchtower with a rifle. I remain agile in mind, and fleet of foot, so you must live with the hope that one day soon you will see and hold me again. Remember we who survived are the fittest. Many perished.

What did I do to deserve this? I simply strayed beyond the compound; I was gathering wood; I caused them no harm. But they took me and hacked bloodily at the cord that bound us together. Moma, do not forget me. I may be far away but I shall return. Pray to our Gods, make whatever sacrifices are necessary, but above all *believe* that I will return and your prayers will come true. Time stumbles. A month in prison is equal to a year of freedom. We use a different calendar. I have fathered a child, but she (it is a girl) and her mother have been sold to a neighboring estate. I may never see them again. There is perhaps more honor in spilling my seed into a man where there exists no danger of fertilization. But I cannot stoop to such baseness. I will return to you a whole, honorable, and clean man. Hold on.

Your son

III

Higher Ground

Irene twisted her body in line with her head. The sky in the window was small. It had started to snow now. Irene frowned and drew a stray hair from her eyes. Winter promised nothing and took much away. She did not like brown leaves. She did not like death. Irene was forever crying. She had developed a habit of letting her chin drop forward so that it touched her chest. Irene sat up in bed. She occasionally indulged in her habit in an attempt to find sleep. Sometimes it worked because in such a position her eyes naturally closed. She liked it with her chin tucked into her chest. It suited her. But sometimes she remembered. ('Don't look so glum, love.' Had he ever heard the low moaning of the wind? Had he ever witnessed men and women and children dressed in fatigue and apathy, unable to register the smallest trace of emotion? Had he, in the theatre of his mind, ever sat through the final drama, 'without self-respect'? 'Don't look so glum, love.' He smiled as Irene stepped from the bus. Then he turned to take more fares. He had meant well.)

Irene's room was small. The frame of the bed was cold and metallic. No matter how warm it might be inside of the bed, the frame was always cold. She dreaded accidentally touching it in the night. She once dragged her mattress on to the floor, but in the morning Mrs Molloy looked at her and wrote something in the black book that she carried with her. Irene hauled the mattress back up on to the frame. In a corner a badly shaded lamp sat upon a small table; in front of the table stood a straight-backed wooden chair. A white porcelain sink decorated the furthest corner, and on the floor a small oval rug covered some of the chequered linoleum. There were no books, despite the fact that a book can neither expel nor despise you. During

175

the day Irene wallowed in surfeit, in the evenings she suffered through denial. She had ensured that there could be no comfort in books.

Irene stepped from the bed and turned on the electric fire. She watched as the two bars hummed into red life, but the fire was dirty and gave off strong fumes. She went to the window and pulled it open. A cat screamed like a child. The lamp-posts had small heads and long necks. Drainpipes climbed up the outside of the buildings opposite. She remembered that her grandmother had once said to her that she would have preferred to have had Irina's time rather than her own. Then she squeezed Irina's hand and told her to be careful. Irene looked at the naked trees, their arms sharp and pointing in all directions. She liked it best when the trees wore clothes, then she would wear hers. The snowflakes spun with a religious monotony that made her want to sing. Instead Irene laughed and imagined God to be shaking a great celestial salt-cellar before he ate up his children. We deserve to be eaten up, thought Irene. We have done nothing good, nothing worthy of him. This will be our last night. The odd car that slushed by, the solitary person leaning into the swirling snow, nobody and nothing would escape the punishment. This was Irene's fantasy, that everyone was deluding themselves, that only the good and the meek would survive, and she knew none who qualified. She was prepared to be shovelled up on to God's spoon and devoured. If he chewed she would bleed. She decided that she would rather drown in his saliva and be swallowed up whole, for people do not like to think of their bodies as bruised and bleeding, especially after their deaths. A stunning or a drowning (so long as the body was removed from the water before it started to decompose), this struck Irene as the best fate that could befall a person. God continued with his shaking. Irene wondered if God had servants who did the shaking for him. Maybe all he had to do was eat, others put the condiments on to his food; he had nothing to do. God is unemployed. He works, but in his own mysterious way. Irene looked at her watch and saw that it was three o'clock. For her sleep was cruel. The mind relaxed and could admit pain. It hurt to sleep,

176

it hurt not to sleep. In the next room a bell sounded. The old man had a rubber sheet that triggered an alarm when he passed water on to it. He had lost control, and then quickly given up the struggle to regain it. Dignity was a little word. Irene laughed, pulled a face, and tried to ease the iron handcuff from around her head. It rested on her temples. She needed to sleep otherwise somebody would soon turn the screw through a further one hundred and eighty degrees.

Irina remembered how Papa's unrequited kisses would burn her cheeks. He would stare back at her, his child with wild bright eyes, unable to touch her through the protective film of her adolescence. And then he sent her away. 'Papa, you hurt me.' The man in the next room cleared his throat with a wet mucus-riddled cough and hurled a shoe against the wall. 'Stop talking to yourself, you crazy Polish bitch.' A few people admired Papa, but the majority disliked him. They thought him parsimonious and unsmiling. They accused him of caring only for himself and his family. Rachel and Irina would sit in the park and exchange anecdotes they had heard about Papa's meanness. About how he declined to give credit to those who wanted to pay it back over one month instead of three. Or how he had discovered sources of foreign supply and then refused to let any other shopkeepers share in his good fortune. Rachel and Irina decided that all of these stories were rooted in jealousy, and that Papa was a good businessman and people were always jealous of good businessmen. Papa had developed a habit of staring at them both, Irina in particular. The two sisters talked about this new affection of their father's, and Irina grew used to feeling his eyes upon her. Then history overwound her time, the spring snapped, and Irina's life ran crazily away from Papa.

In those days an excess of books was the only sign of profligacy that marked the otherwise frugal décor of the flat above the grocer's shop. As Irina grew older she learned to drink their secrets. She could never imagine living in a home where there were no books: Mama and Papa took great pride in her hunger for words. The sound of another page turning meant Irina was sliding deeper into a world from which she would

177

have to be physically shaken. 'Irina! Irina! Can you not hear me shouting? Are you drowning in those words?' As a child the sky held up Irina's kite-dreams, but now her life was grounded. There was no longer a light summery breeze; she never tilted her head to the sun and smiled. As a child she would toss her soul up to the gentle Gods in the knowledge that it would be cared for and returned to her intact. As a child.

Mama was ten years younger than Papa. She seldom spoke about her family except to say that they came from a small village. She claimed that her father died fighting for the Russians against the Germans, and that her mother died of grief. After this double tragedy the villagers took pity on her until it was safe for her to venture forth and seek work in the war-ravaged heart of their new nation. Irina felt uneasy whenever she looked at photographs of her Mama that were taken at this time; the older woman had a pale, foggy face and held herself stiffly. Mother and daughter were as one, there could be no mistaking their lineage. Papa found her. He never said he met her, or fell in love with her, he always found her. Mama once laughed and told Irina that when they first met Papa's sentences always had a beginning and a middle but no end, and Papa overheard and explained that this was because he was so much in awe of her beauty that he was unable to finish a sentence. They said nothing further about themselves as lovers.

Papa's family was less of a mystery to Irina than her Mama's, for his parents, her grandparents, used to share the room next to herself and Rachel. Then Grandfather died, which left only Granny Klara. Neither Rachel nor Irina liked to go into her room for when she became tired she spoke another language and the sisters either pretended to understand her or ignored her depending upon how they felt. If Papa noticed then he said nothing to either of them, perhaps out of gratitude that they were never cruel towards her. Granny Klara, with her funny habits, would have been an easy person to mock. She liked to dig her bony finger into Irina's budding chest and laugh as she told Irina that she was a tree with no roots that a single boy might pick up and toss into the back of a waiting truck. Granny Klara always insisted that they could be taken whole, that there was no need to tug at them, just pick them up, and then the careless tears would appear. Irina could only listen for so long.

And then death broke into Granny Klara's life and she left in her sleep. The previous evening Rachel and Irina had put their heads around the corner of her bedroom door to say 'Goodnight' and Granny Klara had smiled her toothless grin and waved her prematurely skeletal hand. Mama screamed and came hurtling downstairs to join Papa and the two girls at the breakfast table. But Papa must have known for he looked up at Mama, then calmly stood and walked upstairs. Rachel and Irina prepared themselves for school. They too must have known for they did not ask Mama what it was that she had screamed about.

On the way to school Rachel asked Irina what an orgasm was. Irina told her sister to keep her voice down, then she wondered if her Mama had possessed an orgasm when her Papa made her. The sky relaxed and light fell from between the clouds. One day Irina would have a man and know for herself. He would warm her like an old overcoat and she would bathe her lips in the dampness of his mouth. When she returned from school Irina could sense that Granny Klara had already gone. Papa stood in the shop serving customers as though nothing had occurred. A woman stood by the counter and clutched her large bag with both hands. She did not answer when Irina said 'Good afternoon'. Papa went up the ladder. He came down and handed the woman the soap and she threw the coins down on to the counter, smiled sourly, and left. Irina looked at Papa, knowing that he could not be happy, but she could think of nothing she might do to help him. Papa refused to meet his daughter's eyes and he carried on with his chores as though consumed with indifference. Irina left him.

Once upstairs Irina slowly opened the door to Granny's room. She was gone, the bed folded down, the windows opened. Irina wondered when her parents would tell her that this was to be her room. Dinner that evening was clearly intended to be some form of memorial to Granny Klara, but Irina did not want to listen to talk about a dead woman; Papa's words drummed against her deaf ears. Then she saw in Papa's face how her behaviour was upsetting him and guilt rifled through her. Mama smiled at Irina and underneath the table took her daughter's hand into her own. But Irina could think only of the room.

Irene touched herself and remembered that she had mislain her virginity: for a few seconds her mind tried to expunge Reg, but as ever his face returned to trouble her, to remind her that she had twice been abandoned. She looked out of the window where the flames reached to the sky and singed the young snowflakes. 'Why has this happened to me?' she whispered now. In the street below a door slammed. A man flicked up his coat collar and skipped down four steps. He seemed too old to be driving the young car he climbed into. Too old for such dark rendezvousing. Irene turned from the window. She sat naked on the wooden chair. She turned it around so that it faced the electric fire, then she leaned forward and warmed her hands. Next door she heard the snoring of the old man who had once again fallen asleep. But why could she not sleep? Why did she have to continually endure this ritual? Today was Papa's birthday and Irene began to cry. She could not spend another winter in England staunching memories like blood from a punched nose. She could not afford a memory-haemor-rhage, but to not remember hurt. Soon it would be Mrs Molloy and her black book knocking on the door and asking her to be quiet, telling her to be quiet, but why should she? Why? Day soon. Another day.

Irene fell asleep and woke suddenly. She had dreamt that she was deep in a world of warm blackness. Then she had felt an urgent morning call on her face. A mist had enveloped her and she opened her eyes and found herself at the end of an alleyway with blood on her clothes and a light sweat on her brow. Irene reached up and mopped away the perspiration with the back of her hand. Downstairs Mrs Molloy had turned on her wireless and was now singing in a dry tuneless voice that nominally traced the rise and fall of the music without ever complementing it. Neither song nor symphony had formed a part of Irene's upbringing. She owned neither wireless nor

180

record player. They were instruments of pleasure. Irene shuddered and felt a draught gnawing at the back of her neck and circling around her ankles. She stood and picked a towel out of a narrow box-drawer, then padded to the sink where she pinned up her secret hair (that she let down only in the privacy of her own room). She squeezed the single star-shaped tap into reluctant life.

When Irene's watch read nearly eight o'clock her stomach knotted and made a fist. She would have to leave now; there could be no more delaying. She pulled on a large green coat and closed the door behind her. Mrs Molloy's singing voice over-reached and under-achieved. Irene tried not to listen as she eased down the once-patterned stair carpet that now oozed just one sludge colour. She rolled her way around the front door and out into the air that rushed in silently and clouded out in a great steamy performance. For a moment she simply stood and watched. It had stopped snowing. In front of her the morning traffic had already begun to wash by, throwing up an intermittent spray of slush as it did so. A car with a self-consciously melodious horn slowed almost to a halt and Irene turned her head away. It was time to leave. She stepped down the worn, almost concave steps and began to burrow a hole into the kicking wind. She tunnelled quickly and erratically, occasionally squeezing by a shop window that licked her coat sleeve with grime, but Irene did not notice.

Mr Lawrence stood sententiously by the library door. His pock-marked skin was a sallow fish-belly white, and Irene pitied him. She knew he was waiting to see how late she would be. He was one of those doomed people who had not, and would never learn how to conceal their intent. When he tried to be subtle he was crude. For instance, this raw-boned, gangly man, if he wished to indicate that he was angry with Irene he would stare at the facial hair on her top lip, then scratch his recently acquired, razor-thin moustache and smile. Irene pushed past him and into the large warm room that was her place of work. She slipped out of her green coat and hung it up in a corner beside the posters that advertised a range of local services. The posters were so badly hung it looked as though they had randomly

181

jumped up and on to the wall. Irene once tried to straighten them out, but she was told that this was not her job. Mr Lawrence came back into the library. Irene avoided his punitive gaze and began her work re-cataloguing the children's section. 'Mr Lawrence, I'm shipwrecked but alive. I'm no longer willing to share your damp flotsam and wait for the next wave to break and ride with you, at your speed, and in your direction. Look at me, Mr Lawrence, I'm thirty-seven and I can swim. I'm swimming.' Irene closed her eyes. She wondered if it might be possible to stop the wave, to cup it in her hand before it broke, to preserve its curled beauty; to stop swimming for a moment, to sink quietly with grace and dignity.

She opened a book and discovered a looped hair on a page. Irene asked herself what the hair was doing there, and whose hair it was. Her mind could ramble over such thoughts for hours on end. When she returned to her senses she would inevitably find Mr Lawrence staring at her and preparing himself to deliver a lecture that she would receive as words running and racing like rivers, one moment clinging together, the next breaking up into ungrammatical tributaries. Irene would want to cry for he made her realize that her once icicle-sharp mind had melted over the years and she no longer had full command of her senses. She shut the book on the hair and looked up as the first readers began to drift in and sit at the toast-warm table by the radiator. She stared but could not see the man about whom she had spent most of the night thinking, so she continued indexing.

When Irene first worked in England there was a man at the munitions factory who used to stare at her with violence. Mrs McKenzie said that 'up here' there were not many of Irina's 'people', and Irina tried to smile and forget at the same time. The Germans had invaded her country and the war had now come officially to this new place, England. The other young people who had arrived at Liverpool Street Station in London, they were now scattered throughout the country in places as far away as Scotland. It was useless trying to remain in contact with them. As for home, nobody answered her letters and Irina wondered if they arrived at all. Nobody in the London agency could help. Everybody appeared to be in the same dilemma, and Irina was beginning to face up to the fact that she might have to wait and continue to guard the pictures until the war was over. They were her only link with the past.

Mrs McKenzie, hair smashed tight beneath laddered stockings (but Irina knew these were hard times for everybody), suggested Irina should try to find work at the local factory where she would not only meet people but also get a chance to practise the language, which at the moment she spoke slowly and with great difficulty. Mrs McKenzie was anxious that Irina should persevere before her confidence fell away and she found herself swallowed up in silence. As they approached the factory, whose smoke rose straight like an extension of the chimneys, and whose people stared with listless eyes as they poured through the narrow streets, Mrs McKenzie gave her charge a smile and a reassuring squeeze. Irina was not to know but it was now that the Irene-Irina-Irene-Irina-Irene-Irina-Irene problem would begin, for English people were too lazy to bend their mouths or twist their tongues into unfamiliar shapes. The cold sun barely warmed Irina's face and she shivered. Mrs McKenzie stroked her hair.

Mrs McKenzie left Irina with the manager, who stared at her with violence. He escorted her through the large double doors and on to a factory floor that was carpeted with cigarette ends. Irina saw the washers that she would have to box into cardboard coffins. 'Well come on, love, get on with it.' She noticed that the factory girls looked as though they washed their hair in grease. They were dirty. One momentarily took off her headscarf. She turned quickly and her hair lashed in a black whip. Another stood harvesting flakes of dead skin from her hands and casually confetti-ing them about her feet. Irina decided not to show any emotion in front of these people.

He stood over her and chewed gum.

'Hello, my darling. A few of 'em reckon you don't speak no English.'

Irene looked up at his confident face; his cheek-bones were high but well fleshed out. She could see that in later years his skin would be sucked into his mouth and his facial structure would become more prominent, but that would be in time to come.

'Well come on, do you or don't you? You've been here long enough now.'

The girl at the next bench, a buxom matronly woman in her thirties whose husband was away with the Navy, turned to Reg.

'Get lost, creep. Irene's got work to do even if you haven't, so do you mind?'

Reg roared with laughter.

'Get you, Fatty Arbuckle!'

A few men, and some women in earshot, laughed along with him. In a place as miserable as this the most mundane humour provoked overblown gales of laughter.

'What you doing tonight then?' asked Reg.

Crying myself to sleep, thought Irene, a habit that has become as depressingly familiar as washing my face or taking off my shoes. She looked back at this young man; I am abandoned, you do not want me, you mock me. There was silence and Irene felt anxious. Please do not be cruel or unkind to me. I suspect men can manipulate women with words, with hateful words alone. She listened and in her mind somebody nudged a door closed. Irene waited until she heard the long overdue rattle of a bolt being thrust home for the night. Then she opened her eyes and allowed the yellowing glow of a kerosene lamp to creep into her face. She would have to leave now otherwise she would be late, but she would have to be careful. Having passed her eighteenth birthday she would have to open the remaining door herself. Careful. Outside she could hear the wind pursuing small clouds of dust.

'Don't you understand me?'

The buxom woman spoke up.

'Of course, she understands you, she just don't wanna talk to you that's all.'

'She can speak for herself, alright?'

'It's not me who needs telling that.'

Irene put down the cardboard box.

'I'm not doing anything tonight.'

Reg was taken off guard. The pause was almost imperceptible, but he was looking at her and Irene saw the shock travel across his face. He missed a beat but began again with perfect timing.

'Well I'm going out for a few drinks. Want to tag along?'

Irene nodded, but she felt ashamed for all eyes were now upon her. Reg walked off still chewing furiously. Irene felt sure that inside he must be kicking himself. The buxom woman turned from Irene as though hurt, and Irene continued to box.

Reg met her at the end of the day and said he would call for her at eight. Irene said 'no', that she would rather meet him somewhere else and he suggested by the Town Hall. When Irene arrived home she had her tea, as usual, and then told Mrs McKenzie that she would be going out for a drink with some people from work. Mrs McKenzie smiled at her, delighted that at last Irene was finding her own feet. She fussed about and asked Irene if there was something that she could do for her. Irene said there was nothing and she went upstairs and into the bathroom. She ran the bath, stepped into the tub, lay back, and sighed. Today something unequivocally substantial had happened and she had decided to let it occur, it was her decision, she had consulted nobody. Once back in her bedroom Irene towelled herself dry and put on a clean dress. As she pulled down the dress she rubbed her hand along the inside of her thigh.

The moon appeared but was soon obscured again. Irene waited and tried hard not to admit to herself that he had in all likelihood changed his mind. This was her first attempt to emerge from behind the wall of shyness that she knew she would have to leap, or step around, or be hauled over, for she could feel it growing higher by the day: she worried that unless she acted it would one day begin to curl around her and eventually become her brick and mortar shroud. She looked up. The moon was still invisible but the wind was making thin islands of the clouds. And then the wind coughed and in the small park opposite the Town Hall a last leaf fell from a tree in a wide spiral. Reg broke the silence, his shoes click-clacking against the pavement.

185

'Sorry I'm late. Got a bit held up.'

The pub was almost deserted. In the corner two men and a girl, whom Irene recognized from the factory, sat huddled around a small wooden table with their drinks before them. Among their drinks Irene noticed a half-finished glass of beer which she assumed to be Reg's. This was confirmed when he steered her towards the bar and bought a solitary gin, which he handed to her.

Irene muttered her thanks and followed Reg over to the table where his friends were drinking heavily and already spoke with disorganized tongues. They greeted Irene politely, as though instructed to do so, but she knew she was little more than an exotic appendage to their provincial English talk. Irene listened but found great difficulty in reading their conversation. It was easier with just one person. With so many, and especially with people who kept bursting into unadvertised laughter, it was impossible. Occasionally Reg would attempt to slot her into convenient pockets of their gossip, but inevitably he would fail and then laugh mawkishly as he tried to paper over the thin crevices of his now open delusion.

'What do you think, Irene?' was his favourite way of dragging her bodily into their arena, but it was not long before a man rang a bell and shouted 'Time!' and Reg suggested that he drop her back home which seemed to Irene an act of great mercy.

The car was small, but looked new. Irene realized that Reg, or rather Reg's family, must be reasonably comfortable. He drove confidently with one hand on the wheel and the other alternating between the gear-stick and Irene's knee, a constant irritation which made her feel as though his interest in her was solely determined by the changing notes of the engine. Irene looked out of the window and wondered if he wanted to see her again. It had not been a good or even a successful evening, but Reg had made an effort, not a great effort but an effort none the less, one for which she was grateful.

Reg switched off the engine and then the car lights.

'I'm not very good at this,' he announced, as though he were about to perform a service. Before Irene had a chance to ask him what exactly it was that he did not think he was very good at, he leaned over and kissed her on the cheek and then, as though remembering that he had not completed his task, he took her face in his hands and twisted it around so that he could kiss her on the mouth. Irene kept her mouth shut and felt the dry scratching of his lips. She wondered why kisses in films lasted so long, for surely one's lungs must eventually burst. Then Irene felt his tongue, which like a short muscled animal was trying to force its way between her lips, and she pulled away. Reg's voice found a new key.

'Have I done something wrong, love?'

She shook her head, but did not turn her face to meet his.

'You can tell us if I have. I'll not be offended.'

'It's nothing, Reg.'

Irene surprised herself for this was the first time she had spoken his name. That was enough, the evening would end here and she would place it in the lap of the Gods as to whether or not she would see him again. As she stepped from the car Irene muttered 'Goodnight'. She straightened her skirt, then walked through the small wooden gate and up the path towards the house. Irene could see that the lights were still on. She waited until she heard the car leave before she knocked. Mrs McKenzie smiled at Irene and asked if she had enjoyed a good time. Irene said that she had and then went straight upstairs and thought of Rachel and the many times they had spoken of boys.

During the next month Reg asked her out once a week, always on a Thursday, and always to the pub, where more often than not the same group would sit around the same drinks and Irene would listen to new permutations of the same conversation. Irene had not the confidence to suggest the pictures or a walk or some alternative, but she did find the confidence to endure as his hand travelled with surety through the pass between her breasts and then up and over one breast and across and down the other as he mapped the geography of her body and announced each new discovery with a high asthmatic breathing which, after her initial alarm, Irene took as a signal to press her knees tightly together and try to squeeze the inner passion out from its prison. But inevitably she failed. She could sense the shiver of annoyance running through Reg as he turned from her rigid body and started the car engine.

And then one Thursday Reg did not take her to the pub. They drove crazily as the rain drum-rolled against the car. They said nothing. And then Reg stopped in a secluded wooded lane. Irene looked out of the window at the heavily muscled trees. Around their feet the flowers were dying, their heads snapped forward as though tired of attentive life. She heard Reg switch off the engine, and then the lights, and he plunged them both into near darkness.

'I thought maybe we could come here,' began Reg.

Irene reached through the half-light and put her hand on his arm. He stopped talking. She could see that he was nervous, his head crowned with beads of sweat, whole and regularly spaced, as though placed there by an eye-dropper, but there was no need for explanation for Irene was ready to surrender to this man who was the least-worst of those she had known, and the first who had ever shown any interest in her body. Her life had long since taken on the aspect of a dream, and practical proof of her existence, of her continued development, of her worth, was what she needed and this was what Reg had given to her. What she had gleaned about him was simple. He lived at home, loved his parents, and wanted to end up in a white collar in a semi-detached home with his own car, his own wife, and his own dog. Although she did not imagine that she might qualify as a wife he had told her things about his family, his hopes, his past, things she felt sure he would never discuss with his other friends, things that men thought about, fears and secrets that were incompatible with beer and smoke and beards and penises. And naturally enough Irene managed to fake concern, although it was often difficult for she had never had a relationship before and the rules were awkward to discern. How concerned was one supposed to be? How much faking was permissible?

Reg touched her face as though unfamiliar with skin. Irene listened as the rain slapped the leaves and passed judgement with a slow and regular handclap. He moved towards her and

Irene knew already that she would suffer intercourse rather than participate in it. Her legs moved first one way, then the other, then Irene felt her head jammed up against the window in a position more gawkish than uncomfortable. As he searched for her path she grimaced and thought to herself 'careful, please, careful', but then she felt dizzy and sensed the dull trickle of blood (or what she imagined to be blood) and closed her eyes. Reg's wet mouth pressed up against hers and he began to race now, one goal in mind, one receptacle gloved between his hands, his back damp, his backside rising and falling and being tossed about in a storm of its own creation, and then Irene opened her eyes and looked out of the window. She was moved by the painful monotony of this attack to search for faces, car lights, anything, not out of fear but as a sign that she was not dreaming, but Reg hammered on until he broke into high watery breath and a volley of grateful platitudes that Irene was happy to accept. He slid off her and began to gabble with the thickening tongue of a drunk, and Irene wished that he could be quiet for just a few seconds so that she might remember a moment's stillness, but even as he spoke he was hastily re-arranging himself, and then he started the car engine.

Reg drove home slowly in mimicry of triumph. Irene tried to look suitably impressed by the solemnity of what had passed, but in reality she felt grubby and depressingly damp in between her legs where the tide had already begun to turn. Reg whistled. A thrust and a small shudder had changed his personality from that of the actor into the real person and Irene was unsure if she liked either, although she had tolerated the actor in the vain hope that when the playing stopped (which it inevitably would) he might be a nicer person than she suspected. Reg parked the car at the end of the street and Irene decided to try and avoid the embarrassment of any scene which might be even vaguely interpreted as romantic.

'Next week?' asked Reg hopefully.

Irene smiled. Lit only by the street-lights, Reg appeared slightly jaundiced.

'You are alright, aren't you?' asked Reg. 'You did like it?'

Poor twenty-one-year-old Reg, thought Irene. Worried.

Worried perhaps that he might miss his friends at the pub, or was she being unkind? Was he genuinely concerned for her? She thought not.

'I have to go now,' said Irene.

Reg kissed her gently and held her hand.

'You're the tops, Irene, and don't you forget it.'

His performance showed him adopting the role of sympathy, but Irene knew it was an easier part to play than that of understanding. Given Reg's limited range it was perhaps better that he played one of the stock two-dimensional characters that tread noisily across the boards of women's sanity, rather than make a fool of himself in the tragedian's garb.

Mrs McKenzie opened the door and was surprised to see Irene back so soon.

'Come and listen to the wireless with me, love.'

Irene shook her head and dashed straight upstairs. She closed her bedroom door and reached for a handkerchief. As she attended to herself she thought that it was not so much that she felt like a woman, it was just that she no longer felt like a child. She had been entered, filled, and used as a woman: she had attended a rudimentary lecture in desire and, as she suspected, she had found desire a palatable alternative to possession, for if you possessed something, particularly something you wanted, then somebody might come and take it from you and cause you hurt. Her fear was that she doubted if she would ever again have the strength to want to possess, but this fear caused her so much anguish that she quickly flushed it to the back of her mind.

When she returned from the bathroom Irene reached for her nightdress and then changed her mind and tucked it under the pillow. She pulled back the sheet and blankets, and climbed into bed naked. She savoured the crisp coldness of the cotton as it stung all parts of her body. Then she pointed her toes and listened as outside the storm finally broke. That night Irene dreamed of Rachel, who always maintained that she would never marry. They were close, only two years separating them in age, and especially towards the end Irina found herself talking more with Rachel than she did with schoolfriends of her own age. Rachel became a friend before she was a sister.

When Rachel was beaten it affected Irina badly, but the attack was not unexpected. It was Rachel who had once suggested that they should discuss the 'problem' with Mama, but Irina said 'no' for she had noticed that Mama was showing signs of tired resignation, and had formed a habit of speaking to strangers with her eyes lowered, although she still found the strength to allow a smile to attach itself to her mouth when speaking with her daughters. Irina looked at her beautiful Mama and realized that women aged cruelly; that eventually their creases became folds.

Mama bathed Rachel's bruises with iodine and cotton wool. 'Who did this to you?' asked Papa.

Rachel shrugged her shoulders as though completely unmoved by the whole affair, and Mama glanced at Papa as if to say, 'Please do not ask our daughter too many questions.' Papa took both of Rachel's hands in his and he held her tight. Rachel looked up at him.

'It doesn't matter, Papa. I don't want to talk about it.'

Irina stood to one side, disturbed by her sister's reticence. It was only this morning that Papa had made his first concession to the times they were living in. Over breakfast he told both Irina and Rachel that they would not be allowed to go to the university. 'My daughters will never sit upon ghetto benches.' And then Rachel had gone to school, leaving Irina at home to study for her final examinations.

That night Irina abandoned Granny Klara's room and curled up next to Rachel in the big double bed. The light bulb creamed the room a pale yellow and they both breathed deeply and irregularly, for the summer heat hung thick in the air. Downstairs they could hear their parents arguing. Mama shouted at Papa that he was not clinging to history but history was clinging to him. Irina hugged Rachel close and they lay with their arms around each other. Again Mama shouted. She wanted to leave and go away to England or America, for what had happened to Rachel had frightened her, but Papa was against it. Irina looked across at her sister, who was nodding in and out of sleep. She wondered if Rachel would ever achieve her dream of becoming a doctor and resettling in Palestine?

She wondered about the Traditionalists with their beards and prayer shawls and large-brimmed hats and curls at their temples, men who strode confidently to and from Warsaw trams and synagogues, walking so tall and straight that they looked as though they were trying to rub the top of their heads against the belly of the sky. Did they ever suffer fear? Then Irina dreamt that she heard the hush then flutter of migrating birds, and suddenly she was one of them soaring over snow-helmeted mountains, wheeling past winter trees that were frozen into shapes of loudly exclaimed horror, banking away from clouds that hung so low they were in danger of snagging themselves on tree-tops, until she came to rest on a beach by the sea where she intended to let her scars heal. And then she dreamt of a man lying in the gutter, his legs twitching as though trying to shake off tightly fitting shoes. It was not Papa. She did not know the man, but she recognized Papa's favourite pants. Irina woke suddenly and reached for a small mirror which she held to Rachel's mouth. Mercifully it misted up. Then Irina looked into the mirror and felt momentarily grateful that she could not see her own reflection. *Harginnen*. 'They're going to kill us'.

Louis stared at her pale oval face. She had noticed him, that he was sure of, but she worked without looking up, her pen scratching assiduously from left to right. He pushed his shoes against the radiator and toyed with the idea of slipping them off and warming his feet as the other men did, but he worried that his socks might smell even worse than theirs and so he roasted his rubber soles and wished that the material was a less effective insulator. He had been ten days in England with this steel-cold air washing through his lungs. Most of his time had been spent walking the streets and staring at the slabs of colourless concrete that were offset by grey weeping skies. There was no vista to this landscape, no hills, and initially a slow persistent drizzle had cast a mournful aspect over his wanderings; then it had turned to snow, magical and welcome when it first arrived but now chilling him through to his bones. The hostel housed West Indian men who smelt of rain and gas stoves and curtains, and Englishmen who smelt as though they had been playing with dogs. It was against the rules for the residents to remain on the premises during the day so Louis had become a student of the streets, guardedly watching the 'Teddy Boys' (as they called themselves) with their oily hair and nasty smiles; watching women from home who occasionally forgot and carried a bag of shopping on their heads; and, saddest of all sights, watching West Indian men in cafés surreptitiously mixing tomato ketchup with water and creating soup. Only this morning as he trudged out from the hostel he saw an old woman in a church hat who looked at him as though he reminded her of a son or an old boyfriend. She held her chest and whispered to Louis, 'It hurts.' If today was Wednesday, then by Friday Louis would be half-way home and readying himself to begin anew within the compass of his own world.

Louis continued to gawp. There was something about her that marked her apart from the other women. In truth there had only been one with whom Louis had exchanged anything more than a polite 'yes, please' or 'no, thank you', and she had seemed so extraordinary that it was neither wise nor desirable to assume that she represented anything that might be termed 'normal'. It was on Louis's third night in England, when the possibility of a job had been denied him yet again, and he had finally come to terms with the lack of camaraderie among fellow immigrants. A depressed Louis had felt compelled to step out and discover a club or some place where he might throw off the blanket of loneliness that was choking him. Sonny Mac, a small bullet-headed man from Dominica, and one of the more affluent West Indians in the hostel, suggested the 62 Club, and told Louis how to get there. Then Sonny Mac took away his finger, allowed his sunglasses to drop back on to the bridge of his nose, and walked away as though disappointed that he had been made to divulge the location of a place as well-known as the 62 Club. Louis realized that Sonny Mac now considered him ignorant beyond redemption.

The 62 Club was dark and cold. Women conditioned by the penile circumstances danced among themselves while men, back-to-the-wall, liquor-in-hand, cut a solitary response to the music. Louis bought a pint of soil-thick English beer and eyed the women. The one closest to him wore so much rouge it looked as though somebody had slapped her around the face. Her blond hair was stringy and damp with perspiration. A bemused Louis could not understand why West Indians dizzied themselves on the bottom rung of the social ladder in an atmosphere stale from last night's spilt drinks and cigarette smoke.

Half-way through his third pint of beer, and as he mentally prepared to depart, the girl came to Louis and asked if he wanted to dance. He shook his head but she held her ground.

'First time here?'

The roots of her hair were black, the blond mane obviously the product of a bottle. Louis did not answer. She stared at him for a moment, then simply took his arm and asked if he wanted to go. Louis put down his drink and followed her with curiosity, as opposed to lust, as his guiding principle.

Patty turned on the one-bar electric fire, and the room began to steam up as the kettle boiled. Louis watched as she kicked off her shoes and then lit a cigarette. Her toes were misshapen from fashionable but clumsy footwear.

'I smoke only when I'm alone or when I'm nervous. Or in public to be polite, but never in the streets.' She paused. 'You're quite good-looking for a coloured. Most of 'em call you spades but I expect you know that already. People say the stupidest things like you lot run quicker 'cause you've got big nostrils and find it easier to breathe through 'em, stupid things like that.'

Behind the door her dressing-gown hung like a candlewick shroud. From the other rooms in the house Louis could hear the doleful sounds of a child crying while a mother beat it, and somebody scratching another record into place on an overworked gramophone.

'Sugar?'

'No, thank you.'

'I remember the first time I ever saw a coloured, Paki, I think it was. I cried and cried for days. I used to wonder how you lot knew when you were dirty, but I don't think that's why I cried. I was frightened.'

Patty leaned over and placed the coffee on the floor beside him. She sat on the edge of the bed cradling her own coffee between her hands and letting the cigarette dangle loosely from her lips. Louis picked up his coffee and drew a noisy sip.

'You looked like a boxer in the club standing there. I mean not that you were gonna hit anyone, but well-built and waiting, you know. Have people called you names since you've been here?'

'Not really.'

Patty looked surprised and stubbed out her cigarette in a stray saucer.

'"Shine" and "Midnight" are things they call you. Or "Silvery moon", which is slang for coon, but you look a bit strong for 'em so maybe they'll leave you alone.'

Louis continued to drink his coffee through the cracks in her conversation.

'I never had a husband, don't believe in 'em! Still I'm only twenty-eight, do I look it? They're not like dead goldfish, you can't just bung 'em down the toilet. They stick around to give you aggravation, I've seen it often enough and I know what I'm talking about. I used to think it was my fault my parents got divorced but they'd have got on each other's nerves even without a kid. I don't wanna end up like one of those mad women sitting on the tube talking to themselves, I'm too young for that; or as some old whore standing on a street corner waiting for her plumbing to fall out, or for some punter to drop a quid like he's dropped a glove then expect you to pick it up and come around the corner and drop your knickers, not me, mate, no thanks, I'm happy as I am.'

Louis finished his coffee and Patty leaned over him. She pushed her fingers into his hair and eased his head back.

'You know, I like you 'cause when you walk it's as if you own the world, and you smile with your eyes as if you're always happy and ready for fun. Do you want to hold me naked?'

Patty stood and put the latch on the door. Then she began to unbutton her blouse.

'Well aren't you taking anything off?' She sounded hurt.

Louis began to step from his clothes. A naked Patty came to help him.

'What a great colour. I look so pallid beside it.'

She brushed against him and Louis swelled. As he did so he contemplated the price of a few spasms of pleasure.

'That's nice,' said Patty undoing his shirt buttons. 'I wonder what it feels like not to wear clothes at all. You know, so you can go outside in the nude.'

She giggled then led him down on to the bed where they lay together for a moment. Then Patty spread herself. Louis smelt the unwashed sheets and mounted her gracelessly. She pulled him hard into her and folded her legs behind his back.

'What's it feel like?'

Louis did not answer.

'Blond men remind me of women.' Patty laughed. 'Us together make grey together, you ever thought of that?'

Louis exploded into her, shuddering as he did so, and then his body was silent. Again Patty laughed, but Louis could not tell whether it was happiness or mockery that was consuming her. He rolled over to the far side of the bed and turned from her in self-disgust. She reached across and found his hand.

'Here, feel my appendix scar.'

Louis let her guide his hand along the incision, but he wanted desperately to leave.

'I can still feel you inside of me. Do you mind if I touch myself?'

Louis stepped from the bed and walked straight into the bathroom, pausing only to pick up his underpants. He ran the hot water and watched as it clouded the mirror. Then he pulled on his pants and looked down and noticed the dried stains of premature excitement, as though someone had been panning for salt in his cotton crotch. Having washed, Louis re-entered the bedroom and found Patty leaning against the wall with her back arched like a thin white buttress. Using her forehead as a support she had freed her arms and was now exploring between her legs with the tips of her fingers. As Louis dressed she ignored him and concentrated on bringing herself to a noisy climax. Louis finished dressing and admitted to himself that women scared him. A newly radiant and breathless Patty held his arm as he reached for the door handle.

'Why are you going? It's late. Don't you want to stay here?'

Louis swallowed deeply.

'Please tell me the way back to Harrow Road.'

'Why, have you parked your elephant there?'

Patty cackled, then coughed and began to wheeze.

'I'm only joking, Louis. It's a joke, get it?'

It was dawn by the time Louis reached the hostel. He sat on his bed knowing that in an hour he would have to leave and return to the streets. But his mind was made up. He gathered what money he possessed and checked that he still had the address of the ship's company. He was going home, for he knew that it was better to return as the defeated traveller than be praised as the absent hero and live a life of spiritual poverty. He leaned forward and snatched the notice from the back of the door, the notice that told him there was a cooker on the landing, and that he must not leave anything in the room for it may be stolen, and that if he followed the broken lines on the map he would reach the Public Baths which were marked with an X. Through his window Louis noticed that today the thinly veiled sun would fail again. He glanced at his watch; he would soon have no choice but to set forth and begin his wintry tramping ('Watch your step, guv'). Louis screwed up the notice and tossed it towards the far corner of the room. In the street below he heard the high-heeled rattle of a keen young girl rushing to work. Louis smiled to himself. And then he leaned back and began to roar with laughter. So Sonny Mac came here ten years ago and spent his first week in a Clapham air-raid shelter. Sonny Mac was a stupid man. Louis was going home to where his short, but presently experienced, nightmare would eventually distil down into rum stories of the past. This way he could keep the faith.

Irene looked into his crumpled face. He was staring out of the window where once again it had started to snow. She had felt his gaze upon her but was glad that when she finally looked up their eyes did not meet. As usual he sat with the older and more physically destitute English men, attracting curiosity and hostility in equal parts. Mr Lawrence was disturbed by the man and Irene worried that his presence might provoke an unpleasant scene. Propelled by a sense of charity she stood and walked towards him, but the man turned suddenly and looked up at her with a confidence that belied his condition. Irene stammered.

'There's a pub on the corner. Why don't you go in there?'

The man's eyes were slightly glazed over. Then Irene saw Mr Lawrence striding towards her and she turned and faced him.

'Everything alright?'

In his arms Mr Lawrence carried a tall pile of books; he spoke over them.

'I said is everything alright?'

Irene nodded.

At lunchtime Irene walked into the pub under the railway bridge and noticed the dirty carpets and the peeling wallpaper. She did not frequent pubs; like people they were a continual surprise for it was impossible to know the character of one until you were inside, and then it might be too late. He sat in a corner staring into his pint of beer. Irene crossed over to his table. He looked up at her.

'I knew you'd come!'

Irene unwrapped her scarf. Again the man spoke.

'Let me get you a drink.'

He produced a ten-shilling note.

'Orange juice, please.'

'Is that all?'

'That's all,' whispered Irene.

Irene sat and surveyed this dismal place that she had passed every day for the last year without ever summoning up the courage to enter. Now that she had done so it was just as funereal as she had imagined.

The man approached the bar and Irene looked at his back. She sensed that she was right in thinking him lonely, but she would just have her orange juice and go. It would be unkind to capture him, or anybody else, as a friend. He sat back down and placed the drink before her.

'What's your name, if you don't mind me asking? They call me Louis.'

'Irene.'

'That's a nice name.'

Irene did not think so. She lifted the glass to her mouth, took a small sip, and placed it back on the table-top. She tried to make as little noise as possible. He too was nervous, she could see this now. Irene looked around and saw people staring, people who would normally stand at the bar with their backs turned but who now had their heads and bodies corkscrewed around so they could gape directly at them. Irene wondered if the man noticed this. Then she took another drink. It was her turn to break the silence.

'Do you read a lot?'

The man, Louis, giggled slightly and his face brightened up.

'I used to read a few books back home but nothing much. Well, I don't have to tell you that it was just the warm I was after, but if it means you have to read a book to come in then I can read a book.'

Again he laughed and Irene finished her drink and began to button up her coat.

'You're not going already are you? You've only just reached.'

Irene smiled and stood up.

'I just wanted you to know that if it was me you could sit in the library, but it's not me.'

'Maybe,' he paused. 'Maybe you want to go to the cinema with me? But I don't know any picture that's showing.'

Irene looked at him but said nothing.

'The Empire in Leicester Square. That's a big one. Must be something good on there. I can meet you there tomorrow night, if you like.'

Again he paused. He looked into Irene's face.

'Eight o'clock?'

'Alright,' said Irene, 'eight o'clock.'

Louis stood and offered his hand, which Irene shook. Then she turned and marched through the volley of stares and out into the snow. Louis sat down and watched the doors swing back shut. He looked across at the bar where all eyes were upon him, but he held his ground. He had paid for his drink and he would finish it at his own pace and in his own time. In fact, he would order another one. He picked up his glass, downed what remained, and sauntered over to the bar where he asked for another pint of the earthy beer. The barman twirled a cloth which sent towel-driven air into Louis's face. Then the man next to Louis, a small stooping man, addressed the barman in what Louis had come to recognize as an Irish accent.

'There's a lot of colour in here tonight.'

In his mind Louis ducked, then laughed out loud. He paid for his drink and sat back down. Tomorrow would be his last night in England. His boxer's soul remained unbruised.

Irene sat alone in her room and stared blindly at the wall. They had told her nothing about how to deal with men. They had told her nothing about how to avoid men. She felt unsure of what she was doing. She needed protection, to feel safe again, to not see anybody except perhaps this man for he might understand. She would have to decide whether to admit his gestures or let them break against her withering resolve. By what perverse route, she wondered, had she now come to look upon the hospital as protection? That grey pasture of tall willowy women who worked the pillows into a firm bulky support behind your back, the place of tables whose plastic tops were littered with cigarette ash, of doctors who smiled and put one foot up on the bar of your chair. In hospital Irene learned to hate friendships proffered and attempted attachments and imagined love, and she would let nobody touch her. At first she could find nowhere inside that she might curl up, no corner in her soul that she might shelter in. In hospital the mud and the hands and the bread and the train and the wheels turning and the wind and the voices all became unbearably real until she remembered again how to temporarily lose Irina in books. And then she perfected the technique of pretending that the images had receded; she stopped screaming and started answering questions posed, until eventually they offered her a Mrs Molloy ('You'll be alright with me, love') as the gate through which she might pass back out and on to Anna's platform. But now this twelve-months' experience of life beyond the hospital had left her staring at her feet; again they protruded over the edge. There was no longer anybody to pretend to. She cried and feared death. It hurt to sleep. And again she felt the iron handcuff around her head. One last effort. Just to hold on to him. (Had he ever witnessed?) Given her past the unkindest cut of all was that in ten years they had told her nothing about how to deal with men. They had told her nothing about how to avoid men. 'Mr Lawrence, perhaps I'm not swimming.' She stared at her protruding feet.

Irene rocked back and forth on the chair. Careful. She must be careful for although the yolk was poorly the shell remained smooth and perfectly formed. The father who rescued her would have to be as careful as he was strong. Irene did not want to believe or hope (and she did not want to remember but she did not want to forget). Hope, a single pure flame, rose slowly behind her eyes, then an unmarked, peopled, carriage shunted her mind on to a different track. She had travelled first by truck, then by train from Warsaw to Vienna. And then another train had taken her north to the sea. And then the ship.

When they finally boarded the ship a man led them with jailer-like silence through riveted corridors which to Irina's tired eyes resembled long iron coffins. Eventually they reached their cabins, and the ship lurched, and they were soon pounding miles into the thin silken beat of the sea. Irina joined the others on deck and noticed that the ship left a road behind it, and that the young people around her looked frightened. A boy stammered, unable to flick the words off the end of his tongue, and behind him a solitary girl looked out towards the horizon oblivious of the fact that the wind was shimmering her thin dress so that it danced up and down her body like a cloak of fire. In the evening most went downstairs, but Irina stayed on deck and watched the light speckling the water. There was no noise.

The following day Irina looked on silently as inch by inch they edged their way towards England. First the cliffs, then the gently undulating landscape, then the houses and the buildings came into focus. The beachless coastline resisted bravely as the sea forced her weight upon the land, tugging at the outcrops of rock as if trying to drag them down and bury them for ever. But sadly, even as Irina watched, the sea gradually began to lose some of her magic and became little more than a greasy slimy swell that rocked the ship with the same disdain that it tossed the bits of old wood and tin drums and floating litter and other debris. As they eased into the womb of the harbour the sea heaved her dull bulk up against the quayside and Irina had arrived in England, where she knew nobody, with a suitcase and a photograph album (and a feeling that she was being punished), and a mind tormented by the fear that she might never again touch or hold her sister.

The morning after the beating Rachel would not get out of bed. Irina had gone back upstairs to call Rachel to breakfast and had found her sister huddled up with the bedclothes pulled over her head and her thin voice declaring an inability to move. Irina went downstairs and told Papa, who rushed up to Rachel. Moments later he reappeared.

'Go for the doctor.'

Mama moved towards him and took his arm.

'What is it?'

Papa looked worried, then annoyed.

'I said go for the doctor!'

It was the first time Irina had witnessed Papa raising his voice to his wife. Mama silently pulled on her coat and went downstairs and out into the streets to find the doctor.

When he arrived the doctor rubbed Irina's hair as though she were a large dog.

'And how is my pretty little Irina?'

He passed upstairs to attend to Rachel.

Mama took off her coat and sat down. She sighed and ran her hands up and down the length of her tired legs, but she would not meet Irina's eyes. She sat in solitude, her daughter watching her.

When the doctor came back down he told Papa and Mama, in front of Irina, that he thought there was nothing the matter with Rachel.

'There's only one alternative,' he said tapping his finger to the side of his head. Mama snatched her hand up to her mouth.

'It could all be in the mind,' continued the doctor. He was enjoying his performance. 'It's always difficult with young girls, and so many changes to go through.'

Papa pushed his hand deep into his trouser pocket and drew out a wad of notes which he proceeded to count.

'How much for your trouble, doctor?'

The doctor tried to sneak a look at what was in Papa's hand before answering, but Papa caught him. The man chuckled nervously then tugged at his short beard and requested a fee twice the size of that he would normally receive.

'There's the coming out at such short notice.'

Papa did not blink. He counted out the money into the doctor's hand and bade him farewell. Mama escorted the doctor downstairs. It was now midday and Irina understood that she would not be expected to go to school again. She wondered what she would do? How would she occupy the time? Presumably Rachel needed to rest so it would not be possible to talk with her. Then Mama returned and sat down. Irina waited for her to say something but it was Papa who spoke.

'I think you should go and sit with your sister.'

Irina got to her feet and left without protest.

Rachel was asleep. She did look slightly pale and Irina began to hope that Rachel was ill with something physically definable, like mumps or chicken-pox, so that they might prove the doctor a fraud. It was only when Irina saw her sister staring across at her that she realized she must have fallen asleep. Irina rubbed her eyes.

'How long have I been asleep?'

Rachel laughed. 'I don't know.'

Irina could see sunlight in the street where the day was still full. She looked back at Rachel, who was smiling as though the sisters were sharing a secret.

'Why are you not at school?' asked Rachel. 'Are we not allowed out any more?'

Irina shrugged her shoulders. Then she climbed to her feet and decided to leave Rachel alone.

'Do you want me to bring you anything from downstairs?'

Rachel coughed.

'Yes please. Can I have some water?'

Irina leant forward and gave her sister a kiss on the cheek, a big kiss like she imagined a man's kiss would be.

Mama was sitting at the kitchen table looking through the book which held the family photographs.

'Are you alright, Irina?'

'I'm just getting a drink of water for Rachel.'

Papa was counting money and bundling the notes into envelopes. He stopped what he was doing.

'Is she looking any better?' He did not wait for an answer before turning to Mama. 'Surely she should have some food now? She will need something to build up her strength.'

Mama stood and moved over to the cooker, and Papa addressed his eldest daughter.

'There will shortly be many changes to our life, but I imagine you must have guessed this already. You see, your Mama thinks we should leave before things get worse and maybe she is right. Perhaps when you have taken Rachel her drink you will come back down and help us. It will involve you. It is only fair that you have a voice in whatever it is that might happen to us.'

Irina took the water to Rachel and left quickly with the guilt of one who is betraying another. Papa urged her to sit before him. Irina pulled up a chair and listened to her father, who spoke quietly but firmly.

'In times such as these we can only live for so long in a state of self-deception, am I making myself clear?'

Irina shifted awkwardly on her seat and then nodded.

'Perhaps it is not right for this country to be free,' continued Papa, 'we are not used to it, and we are making a mess of everything. Government, press, church, it is everybody now. Nobody wants to live among people and merely survive, but the Bundists they frighten me with their unhistorical socialism, for only God can lead us to Mount Zion and they will live to discover this.'

Papa stood and poured himself a glass of schnapps.

'While others may pretend it is "business as usual", the evidence of your sister is too much. I think it best that your mother and yourself and Rachel go first. I have money, we will begin again elsewhere, it is not a tragedy.'

Mama spoke up, her voice steady if not confident.

'No, we all go together or at least Irina and Rachel will go first.'

It was clear that Mama was merely carrying on a long-standing argument, and Papa was annoyed that she was airing their disagreement in front of Irina. Mama, however, was not going to give up.

'I refuse to leave you behind, I don't care what you say. We will go together as a family or the children will go and I will wait with you. It is not right that you should remain on your own.'

'Then they must go ahead of us,' said Papa, 'for it will take some time to clear up our business and sell the shop.'

Mama drew in her breath, paused, then burst with frustration. She threw down a wooden spoon.

'Sell the shop! What do you mean sell the shop? Who will buy the shop from us, please let us be sensible about this. The shop will have to look after itself. We cannot be bothered with such things.'

At this point Papa turned away, realizing that he would have to stop the argument. Mama eyed him and then reached over and held her daughter's hand.

'Many families are leaving to go to America and some to England. We think it will be better if we go to England, at least to start with. Your father does not think they will become involved if there is to be a war.' Mama smiled. 'Your English has always been good. At least that's what your teachers tell me.'

Irina hugged her mother.

'We will make all the arrangements for you,' said Papa, 'but it will be soon. It will be as soon as your sister is better and able to travel, but you must say nothing to her.'

Irina wanted to protest. How could they ask her to keep all this from Rachel? If they were going then surely Rachel had a right to know? Mama released her daughter.

'Go upstairs now. Your Papa and I have more to discuss.'

Irina woke at the dead of night and heard a woman sobbing in the next room. Obviously her parents had continued their argument and it had upset her Mama. Downstairs she could hear Papa listening to the wireless. He generally tuned into the foreign stations and tried to obtain as much news as he could from around Europe. Papa spoke a little English, some German, and of course, Polish. Irina seemed to remember that he could also understand some French. When the friendlier of the customers stopped for a conversation, Papa liked to show off his knowledge of these languages by informing them of what was happening in the different countries. Papa's pronouncements always ended with the words, 'Of course, it all means war.' He knew that people thought his talk of war was nonsense but he was happy in the knowledge that he would be one day proved right. Irina cuddled up against Rachel and fell asleep to the sounds of her Mama's sobbing.

Next door she heard the old man preparing himself for bed. Irene turned from the wall and looked out of the window. As ever she was finding it difficult to sleep. It was still snowing. The blanket must be inches deep by now, she thought, deep enough for small people to get lost in it. Then she laughed. The old man banged the heel of his shoe against the wall.

'Stop your laughing, you crazy Polish bitch!'

A week after Mama had sobbed her way through the night everything seemed to have calmed down. Rachel was still in bed, but Mama and Papa went about their daily routine in the shop and in the flat, and Irina was left to read. She was encouraged to go out only in the company of one or both of her parents, so gone were the long walks in the park with Rachel, the fooling about after school, and the sneaked tram rides without a ticket. Gone were the afternoons sitting in the square watching people promenading by, the detours into the Catholic church to stare at the icons, and their wandering through the narrow streets and cobbles of the old town. Winter began to close in, and the wind whipped through the loose-fitting window frames, and Irina spent most of her days upstairs curled up with a book. And then it was Rachel's birthday, but there was nothing pleasant or joyous about it for Rachel was still confined to bed. The doctor was recalled and he repeated his diagnosis, but this time for less money. He insisted that they take Rachel out for a walk, but Rachel would have none of it. Irina and Mama tried for over an hour to persuade her, but she refused to move. Three days later Mama told Irina that Papa was having trouble obtaining the relevant papers, and that he would probably have to buy them at an exhorbitant price, but Irina was not to let him know that Mama had told her this for it would cause him embarrassment.

'I think,' continued Mama, 'that you and Rachel may have to go first. It is not something that we want but according to your father it will not be long before we are the next Czechoslovakia.'

And then suddenly life ended. Irina looked across the breakfast table and noticed her Mama's silence. She assumed that her Mama was recovering from another argument with Papa. When a depressed-looking Papa entered the room Irina imagined her thesis to be correct. But she was wrong. Papa sat heavily and looked at her.

'When I have finished what I am about to say you will go upstairs, pack your small suitcase with sensible things, and then come down here in your overcoat ready to leave.'

Irina felt numb with shock.

'I have managed to place you with a children's transport. You will travel to Vienna and then on to England. That is where we will meet you. Rachel and your mother and I will come on after, but you must leave now. Irina, please go upstairs and get your things and do not make it harder for us.'

She stood up. And then Papa spoke again.

'I think it will be better if you say nothing to your sister. She is not going to become any healthier for the knowledge that you are leaving us. We will tell her after you have gone.'

Irina began to slowly pack her things, putting in books and papers and trinkets and then, realizing that it might take some time to reach England, she began packing again, this time cramming more practical objects into the suitcase and hoping they would all fit. As she moved to go downstairs Irina paused outside Rachel's door, but she dare not enter in an overcoat and carrying a suitcase for this would arouse a suspicion that no amount of devious lying would palliate. So Irina stood and, without understanding why, she found herself praying; she found herself praying that Rachel might find it in her heart to forgive her this sinful departure and that they might soon discover themselves together again.

Irina stared at a seemingly unrepentant Papa, already feeling as though she did not belong in this house. She looked around but there was no time to say goodbye to all the nooks and crannies and little things that she had grown up with. She waited for her instructions and tried to act like an eighteen-year-old adult.

'Irina,' began Papa. He produced a large paper bag. 'We would like you to take these and look after them carefully. They are our photographs and it is better you keep them safe with you.'

Irina took the package and shuffled awkwardly as all three fell into a cavernous silence. Papa looked at his watch.

'I'm sorry, darling, but we really must go.'

He glanced across at his wife and Irina knew that she was now expected to say goodbye to her mother. Mama began to sob, and Irina took the distressed woman in her arms but there was nothing that she could say or do that was going to arrest her mother's misery so she thought it best to break away.

It was a bleak morning. The cold rushed quickly through Irina's city. Then the sun caught bits of broken glass that lay on the road and suddenly the day seemed brighter. At the market square people looked on and laughed as the dozen or so children huddled together with their suitcases and parents. Irina recognized somebody from school and two others from the neighbourhood, but this was not the time for bridge-building; everybody was locked silently into their own private world.

Eventually the children were encouraged to present themselves to the man with round wire-rimmed spectacles who simply ticked off their names on his clipboard. Money had already changed hands and it was understood that they were all privileged. To show too much emotion was to admit that you might never again see your family and friends. Words were difficult. Papa hugged Irina and then took one step back and looked at her.

'Thank you,' was all Irina could think of to say to him. It seemed curiously formal, but somehow appropriate. 'Thank you, Papa.'

Papa looked back and smiled.

'Take care of yourself, Irina. It will not be long now.'

His voice became heavier as he spoke. Irina could see Papa fighting off anger and hurt, wanting her to know that he would have no more room in his heart because of her going. His struggle was transparent. She could also see that he did not want her to remember him without a smile on his face.

Irina was ushered on to the back of the truck. She knew that she should not turn around. Very few of her fellow passengers cricked their necks, for the future that lay ahead of them was already as great an area of concern as the past they were leaving behind. So out and over the cab of the truck they stared, concentrating on going forward, escaping, but even as they did so they realized that a deep guilt was being fused in their souls, a guilt that would be exposed were they now to falter and turn and look back.

After fitful bouts of sleeping Irina woke to hear the roaring of hooters. It was dark, and the train was being shunted into a dockside terminal dominated by the shadows of high cranes. And then the sky began to clear and Irina realized that she was looking out at the sea. She had never before seen the sea, and even from the dockside its expanse filled her with awe. She was really leaving. Her stomach felt uneasy as she reflected on how the travelling of the last few days had obscured her many girlish years and replaced them with womanish hours. Then she withdrew the photograph album from its hiding-place and lay her palm against the front cover. It was still warm.

Irene stood up and walked over to the door. Her room was one of those that never seemed to get any brighter when a light bulb was switched on. She picked up a towel and crushed it into her face. A wheel turned slowly in the cloying mud, faces smiled, and bread was passed from hand to hand. Irene pulled back the curtain, rubbed a round porthole, and peered down into the street. Nothing. She would try to survive this day.

The woman stabbed out another cigarette and turned towards her. Irene continued to look down at the space between her splayed feet. Then she ran an idle hand up and through her hair and laughed at the overscented charm of her visitor.

'Poor girl,' thought the woman, and Irene flashed her a look as though she had read the woman's mind.

'Isn't there anything else you'd like to tell me?' asked the woman. 'You said you'd be happy to talk about your father. Do you want to talk about him?'

Irene leaned forward and flicked on the second bar of the electric fire.

'Cold?' asked the woman.

Irene did not answer so the woman continued.

'At least you don't have to go out to work any more.' She paused. 'I'm sorry, Irene, but the library was only temporary. Some things just don't work out, and if he doesn't want you then that's how it must be. I'm sorry I had to be the one to tell you.' Again she paused hoping that she might have provoked Irene into a reaction, but Irene displayed only the crown of her head where, if she were a man, a bald patch would one day begin to appear.

'Look, love, after nearly ten years in hospital we were lucky to get you anything. People are very funny.'

Again she paused.

'You are cold, aren't you?'

Irene rubbed her hands together but said nothing. The woman swallowed deeply.

'You know you'll have to come back to us. It's not only the library, there's your landlady as well. That's not working out either, is it, love?'

Irene laughed, and then looked up at the woman. She had a slim anorectic face. Irene wondered what tragedy had befallen her that she was now reduced to asking others about their lives as opposed to living her own. Overwhelmed by pity, Irene stretched out a hand and touched the woman on the knee.

'Would you like a cup of tea?'

The woman cupped Irene's hand in hers and pressed down. 'No thank you, Irene.'

Irene retrieved her hand, knitted it loosely into the other one, dropped them both into her lap, and smiled benevolently. The woman's eyebrows arched in confusion.

'What about your husband? Do you miss him?'

Irene closed her eyes. 'What about your husband?' she repeated to herself. It was over ten years since Irene had travelled down to London and tried to throw herself under the train (like Anna Karenina) and been taken into hospital (but not for her bruises). She had not seen Reg for over ten years. Reg, who when he finally accepted the fact that she was pregnant gave her a ring. ('It's easy to fool a young girl, but I never thought it'd come to this.') Irene moved into a flat with him. She spent hours gawping into the mirror at a plain girl who stood behind a pregnant stomach that threw her centre of gravity out in front of her and caused her lower spine to curve inwards as though somebody had put a boot into the small of her back. Her body was often numb with pain, her movements heavy, and she would trudge the streets, occasionally stopping and staring and wanting to scream in the vain hope that things might be different when the scream died away.

The war had ended and Reg had changed. He had a new job but he wasn't 'pulling his weight'; when he moved out of earshot they called the ex-consciencious objector a 'coward'. He would soon be a father but Reg no longer felt like a man. He worked off his fantasies and frustrations by spitting words at Irene. He argued to kill. He often asked Irene to cry quietly, then he would be apologetic and offer her money, then he would order her to cut off her hair. It was too late for Irene to consider the abortion that she had never seriously considered, and so she decided to avoid mirrors. She could feel the head-ball ripening inside of her. Reg kept saying that things would get better, which meant his suits would improve as his waist-line thickened, but when Irene lost the child, and Reg touched her arm and went off to the pub, she knew that she would soon have to leave. A fag-end that needed stubbing out, their marriage had smouldered for long enough. 'Reg, I think I've lost sight of what your normal behaviour is. I can't remember the you I knew before the arguments.' Reg did that grunt-laugh and slammed the door behind him.

Mrs McKenzie had already left and with her had gone the photographs. She had shouted at Irene and told her that she was a refugee who had lost everything but her accent and that she should have been more grateful. And then she calmed down and took Irene's arm and said that she had no drink in the house for she was a Christmas drinker only, but if she had some then she would have poured Irene a whisky. She also told Irene that before she left for the Dales ('to retire') she would leave her things safe with a neighbour, but Mrs McKenzie must have forgotten, and Irene never traced her belongings. So, when she left Reg, or ran away to London, she left and arrived in what she stood in. Then, in the middle of King's Cross station, she remembered Anna and at twenty-six she saw a way of slamming shut her own door, but all she did was open up a new door to this woman and others like her. The grey pasture beckoned.

The woman's voice touched her from afar. She was eager that they should travel further along their conversational straight road, but the idea depressed Irene for she knew that the longer they did so the more chance there was that they would soon come to recognize their old sentences flashing by in both directions. Irene got up, poured water into the teapot, and listened as an ambulance blew past in the street below. The woman reached out an arm and extinguished another cigarette.

'If I understand you better then maybe I can help. You seem to me a remarkable woman in many ways.'

Irene knew that she was being paid the excessive compliment meant only to remind her of who she was.

'Why don't you talk to me, love? Go on, try. I mean happy people don't try to harm themselves, now do they?'

'I don't know,' said Irene, 'I don't know any happy people, do you?'

Irene put down the teapot and laughed. The woman looked

212

alarmed, and then there was a sharp knock at the door. Mrs Molloy stared as Irene rocked back on to her haunches and then slumped down in the corner of the room with tears of laughter spilling out on to her cheeks.

'She'll be alright,' said the woman visitor. 'I'll take her tomorrow'.

'Take me where tomorrow?' cried Irene. She snatched her breath. 'Where are you taking me?'

'I told you, Irene, you'll have to come back.'

'Get out!' roared Irene, as she tried to get to her feet.

Mrs Molloy turned and left. The woman visitor put away the cigarette she had not yet lit. She pulled on her coat.

'Please don't do anything silly, Irene. We're only trying to help.'

'Get out!'

'We'll see you in the morning.'

Irene banged the door shut and leant against it. No. Again, the tall willowy women. No. And nowhere inside where she might curl up. No. She thought of women visitors who dreamt only of careers and babies, babies and careers, drugging their minds with schemes whereby one might complement the other while Irene knew full well that girlish dreams were just that and men have a different way of behaving even if it might take some women marriage to find this out. A whistle sounded and the train jerked forward, the carriages nudging into each other, and then the train began to settle down. The flame from the oil lamp jumped, despite the protection of the glass chimney, and Papa tuned into the BBC for his news. Irina slumped down on to the floor and sobbed for on the wall of the synagogue somebody had chalked a poem which began, 'He who strides ahead of history with a gun is bound to perish', and she could not fathom the poem's meaning. As she walked in the park Irina noticed that she was trampling on a brown carpet of rotting leaves. The air was redolent with a stale perfume that stung her nose, while underfoot she could occasionally feel the cold hard concrete where the carpet needed repairing. Irina sat and stared but nobody would catch her eyes, and so she lay flat out on the bench and in her mind she watched as a glass sailed towards a mirror in a long wide arc. 'Rachel!'

Irene broke sharply to the left, scattered a flock of pigeons, and struck out with authority across a crowded Leicester Square. He was standing calmly by the uniformed attendant. Irene looked at him, smiled, and felt gloriously alive. Light filled the darkness. Louis held her hand throughout the film, and Irene did not remove her headscarf. Afterwards they walked by the river and Irene thought that only the strongest men could survive the glares of disapproval that he pretended not to notice. She looked at London's bright reflection on the surface of the Thames, and then they stopped at a bridge and without consulting him Irene threaded her arm through his and began to cross it. Half-way across she broke free and leaned over the edge.

'I miss the sound of hidden water,' said Louis, thinking of the streams and waterfalls he would soon be reacquainting himself with. They both looked down. The water curdled in tight, almost mean wavelets then continued to flow.

'What about your parents?'

Irene laughed.

'I never had any parents.' She paused. 'Is there something wrong?'

Louis felt bold enough to slip an arm inside her coat and then around her waist. Her body was soft and fleshy, toy-like, but just beneath the surface he could discern the firmness of youth. 'My God,' he thought, 'she must have been beautiful once.' Irene looked up at him and wondered what it was that was stopping him from kissing her. He smiled.

'Where is your accent from?'

Irene laughed out loud and rolled forward on to the tips of her toes. Without leaning on him she placed her lips against his, and then she fell back flat on to the soles of her feet. Louis's eyes travelled along the Thames towards a sister bridge.

'Tomorrow I cross the water again. I should have told you this.'

Irene laughed on, but inside her chest she could feel her heart pumping noisily. Louis continued.

'I'm going back to where I come from.'

Again Irene leaned forward and kissed him. Then she walked away and gestured loudly.

'Let us lie in your sun and allow the scars time to heal!'

She burst into laughter and twirled. It was getting late and the cold wind had broken cover. It raced through the streets, along the river embankment and up and over the bridge. Across the road a man passed by with his anorak securely zipped and his chin dipped low in mute acknowledgement of the bitterness that was winter.

'You're leaving me!' cried Irene, as though the truth of his words had only just reached her. The man across the road did not break step. Louis laughed nervously and again Irene began to twirl. Then she stopped and gasped for breath. She rushed the half-dozen paces towards Louis and roped her arms around his neck.

'Come to my room and let's celebrate.'

Louis kissed Irene on the forehead.

He quietly followed her up the unlit staircase. They turned three gloomy landings before they reached the top, where the roof was lower than on the other landings. Irene giggled, then squashed her hand to her mouth as she pushed open the door and ushered Louis inside. She pointed towards the wooden chair, and then she stopped laughing and turned on the electric fire. The bars hummed pink and then red, and Irene picked up a cup and ran some water into it. Louis glanced around the bare room and sensed an atmosphere at least as depressing as that of the hostel. He turned and caught Irene staring at him.

'Your mouth is always wet. That's nice.'

As she spoke Irene held the cup, but she did not notice that water was spilling out on to the floor. And then she noticed.

'I'm sorry,' she said. 'Let me sit for a moment.'

Irene crouched with her back to the door. Then she looked up and smiled at Louis, who shivered and inched closer to the fire.

'Shall I turn on the light?'

She did not wait for an answer. Her hand snaked up the wall, flicked the switch, and then slid back down. She illuminated her features so that Louis might see her better. The light

215

on her face was a lesson, a book that she hoped he would want to read, but he looked away from her. Irene closed her eyes. It was cruel of her to attempt to make a friend. Still, it would soon be over. But she did not want this man to leave her alone. He was kind. And she feared the loneliness of dreaming, whether asleep or awake, the dreams, in particular the dream of her Mama who ignored her and walked past her in the street, her eyes moving neither left nor right nor up nor down. Irene's Mama walked on callously and left her daughter rooted to the ground. 'I've never seen that coat before,' thought Irene. 'It suits her.' Then she shouted, 'Mama!' but no words came from her mouth and her Mama was soon swallowed up by the tight curve of the street. In her dream Irene always made her way back to the house which held the room that she called 'home', and all night the streets would report to her the repetitive news of dogs barking, breaking glass, and hateful people.

Louis looked across at Irene's face, her mouth open as if she were going to say something, her black hair falling out of its tight bun. He realized that she was one of those women who look older than they are when asleep, but his fascination with her would not evaporate. His tired mind now grappled with the problem of how to go forth and retrieve his own life. He had already decided not to become one of those who expects, like a child expects from a step-mother, but who meanwhile waits as his long fingers turn rusty and his features become contorted into a factory-face; yet he looked at her and sighed, not sure of what it was that he wanted of this woman. Companionship? A friend? She touched him, but he knew that he must steel himself and step out into the crisp, sweatless, fresh, cold, white, snowy night and walk back down to the river so that he might witness the day break over this great city of London. Then at dawn he would return to the men's hostel and take his bag and his leave. It was probable that this woman would extend and demand a severe loyalty that he could never reciprocate. Not now. Sorry.

Irene opened her eyes and looked up at him. His worried face was tram-lined like the shell of a walnut, but she could see that he was trying to look kindly upon her. She stretched out her hand. Around her wrist she wore the thin bracelet of attempted suicide.

'Louis?' She spoke to herself now. 'You say your name is Louis. I try not to go back in my memory for I have spent a small life writing unanswered letters, do you understand?' Irene laughed out loud. 'If you could lick my heart, Louis, it would coat your tongue in salt, a strong and bitter taste. I keep seeing a girl (not I) making up her face, preparing herself for her first date.' Irene paused. The single cautious flame rose and then flickered and then died.

'Can we go now?'

Tears began to spill from her eyes for Irene knew that her life was finally running aground.

'In my mind I can't keep anything quiet.' Irene smiled weakly. 'Tomorrow I have to go back, I can't even keep myself. No library. No more. And this time books won't help. I can't forget Irina.' She paused. 'You don't know her.'

Louis stood and moved uneasily from one foot to the other. He caused the loose floorboards to fire off a volley of timber shots, and Irene stared at him. She climbed to her feet and moved away from the door.

'I'm sorry if I caused you suffering,' whispered Irene.

Louis grasped the door handle. He looked at her but she would not meet his eyes. He spoke softly.

'I'm sure everything will be alright. Just don't worry so much, that's all.'

Irene heard him move quickly from the room and then gently close the door behind him. She went to the window and watched as he stepped down on to the white blanket. He stopped as though he was going to turn and look back up at the window, but then he changed his mind and began to walk through the snow towards his sun.

'*A gite nacht.*' Irene paused. '*Uf widerzain.*'

She kicked off her flat shoes, balled up her feet until the bones cracked, and then stretched them out again. Irene sat on the wooden chair, arched her neck over the back and tossed her head from side to side, at first steadily and with metronomic precision, and then with more abandon as the scream became higher. In her nightmare there was never any air. Bolted, suffocating, and trying to survive a journey. Then they waited and wept and asked for water. To be burned not buried, to have to wait for a high wind. And then a scattered peace. Then total silence. Nothing moved. And the new people began to wonder. *Harginnen.* 'They're going to kill us.'

Irene fell from the chair and bruised her elbow as she punched out an arm to break her fall. Her funny-bone sang and she bit then sucked the fleshy part of her forearm with her irregular lips (that Papa said reminded him of a crushed flower) until her teeth began to cut. Then Irene reached out and grabbed the hem of the curtain and pulled and watched as it popped slowly from its moorings and tumbled to the floor. Now that she had undressed the window she could see the snow falling against the black sky and she cried out, fearful of the long night ahead, more fearful of the morning, for ever lost without the sustaining love.

'Shut up, you crazy Polish bitch.'

The heel of his shoe drummed against the wall. Irene wrapped herself in the curtain and waited patiently for either the new day or the woman visitor, whichever one arrived first.

'Hear, O Israel: the Lord our God, the Lord is one.'

A STATE OF INDEPENDENCE

This sardonically funny and often lyrical novel tells the story of how one exile's homecoming stands in for an entire region's transition from the smothering blanket of colonialism to a dubious state of independence.

Fiction/Literature/0-679-75930-1

THE FINAL PASSAGE

An affecting and haunting tragicomedy about "the final passage"—the exodus of black West Indians from their impoverished islands to the uncertain opportunities of England.

Fiction/Literature/0-679-75931-X

Available at your local bookstore,
or call toll-free to order: 1-800-793-2665
(credit cards only).